The Blind Vampire Hunter

by

Tim Forder

Published by
Melange Books, LLC
White Bear Lake, MN 55110
www.melange-books.com

Cover Art by Stephanie Flint

The Blind Vampire Hunter
Tim Forder

Jack Poisner is legally blind; growing up in a world not yet familiar with the concept of legal blindness, he learns how to fight to survive his peers, the education system and more.

Eventually, happily married with a family of his own and living well with his visual disadvantages, life throws him an overripe pumpkin – when he wakes up one morning and discovers, he is suddenly, totally blind!

As he is adjusting to his new life of visual darkness, a new and much greater darkness enters his life; a boarder, a vampire, that only he can "see", has come to live within the safety of his home, in easy reach of his family and himself.

A vampire hunter is born—The Blind Vampire Hunter

ACKNOWLEDGMENTS
I would like to thank my good friend from John Hopkins...

Gislin Dagnelie, Ph.D.
Associate Professor of Ophthalmology
Lions Vision Research & Rehab Center
Johns Hopkins Univ. School of Medicine
For his technical support pertaining to RP.

Thanks to
James (Digger McGee) Forder
For his technical support on the handling of the newly deceased.

I would like to thank my whole family for their support in this endeavor.

Table of Contents

Introduction

Mardi Gras. A vampire's holiday. For about a week, a vampire may be seen in public, exposed fangs and all; within this massive crowd of festive customers that may include hundreds of costumed vampires. A real vampire is just one more costumed vampire. I'm just another phony costumed vampire among parades of phony vampires, so they assume. If the vampire dines smartly they may have all they can consume without raising any alarms. A vampire's buffet. Drink a little here, consume a little there and with a little restraint no one is hurt, no one is the wiser. The ability to consume without killing takes maturity that only comes with many years of vampire experience.

How old am I? You should know better than to ask a woman her age, especially a female vampire who might forget herself and rip your head off, and gorge on all that delicious blood pumping out of your open neck hole; all that delightfully delicious blood that is supposedly heading for your head to feed your now dying brain. Meanwhile, you are horrifyingly watching this exhibition while your brain is waiting to starve to death.

With everyone in festive clothing and vampires such a popular mythical creature to mimic in costumes, a vampire can come out as they are; even while baring one's real vampire fangs in public, everyone else just thinks you're so cool or just one of hundreds of other costumed vampires.

Hell. A vampire may eat right out in the open and everybody around is thinking you are either over playing your part as a mythical creature of the night, or you are a loving couple too cheap or too cheesy to get a room.

1

"Hi, babe, I got something for you to bite," interrupted my musings. A big fat guy in a biker costume had called out or maybe he really was a real biker. What did it matter? I could sense the increased blood flow pumping hard within this guy. Apparently my sexy vampire outfit consisting of a white off-the-shoulder peasant blouse with red lace, short black skirt, and of course, the ever present Vampire black satin cape with red interior was already getting this guy's juices flowing, already seasoning his blood with delicious endorphins. *My next meal is about to be served.*

Walking seductively toward him, creating a nice little wave of my skirt and a nice bounce from within my braless peasant blouse, I deliberately walked up to him in a way that would further turn him on and get those spicy endorphins flowing. As I got close to him, I made eye contact with my appetizer, my first meal of the night. This just got his juices flowing faster; he was going to be a good first meal...

He was not properly prepared yet so, tantalizingly him further, I whispered, "And I have something for *you*," while giving him a little private squeeze of a growing bulge below the belt as I spoke. That did it; if he got any more excited, he might give himself a heart attack. He was just about ready.

As I locked my gaze with his, I put the thought into his over-sexed mind that he was about to get the hickey of his life. After giving him a light feathery kiss on his lips to give him something to think about, I brushed my luscious lips down and sideways on to his neck. When I found the strong pumping vein I was looking for I sunk my fangs into his neck and totally orgasamed on my first meal of the night. Personally, I favor my meals heavily seasoned with endorphins, easily done with a little sexual foreplay, but I'm not likely to pass up a meal nicely seasoned with adrenalin even easier to create from a heavy dose of fear.

As I dined, a clown passing by called out, "Get a room!"

This was early into this night's festivity. Later in the night, there would be so many lovers necking, everyone else will just begin to unconsciously ignore it, especially those who have gotten into the local joy juice. [There is some fine liquor in Louisiana.]

I left the biker resting up against the wall; he looked as if he had just had the best part of this night, and yes, he was very much alive. With all the dining opportunities tonight would provide, there was no need for anyone to die, particularly if I could enthrall them into total bliss as easily as I enthralled that biker.

At one point in the evening, I heard a voice from above calling, "Lady Vampire, up here, Lady Vampire." Looking skyward, I found a man calling down to me. He looked as if he might really be a fellow vampire in his smashing leather suit and beautiful long ivory fangs. He had fangs a Vampire would undie for. He called down, "Room 410, come up and see me." So I did.

As I neared the door with the gold number "410" embossed on it, the door opened and the fellow vampire...was a phony. He had a heartbeat and, from down within the crowd, I was not able to detect any sound of a heartbeat. I really thought he might be the real thing, a fellow Vampire out to enjoy the Vampire smorgasbord this night provides. He waved a gentlemanly arm and proclaimed, "Please, fellow Vampire, come in, come in."

My disappointment in finding my Vampire host to be a phony must have shown. "Is there something wrong?"

Well, this would provide for a nice quiet, undisturbed meal, so why not.

Painting a smile on her face, she entered saying, "I am surprised to see that you have two beds in your gentleman's suite." It seemed odd to me that a single man would pay for a room with two beds. I have had some experience within many gentlemen's hotel or motel rooms, so this really seemed odd.

With a slightly leering look, my phony Vampire answered, "One bed to exercise with my quests and one bed to sleep on."

I noticed that one bed had indeed been used, the thrown off sheets made it easy to surmise that it was not used for sleeping. My next meal was making his way toward a table with two chairs conveniently placed so one or more could easily take in the festivities below. He showed me a seat and said, "Please sit and enjoy the view while I get us a couple of drinks from the min-bar. Would you like a wine or a beer as we enjoy the festivities above the hubbub of the crowds below?"

"Just water, please." When I entered, I noticed an increase in the sound of his beating heart. From many years experience I knew for a fact that my next appetizer was already starting to season up nicely with his premonition of a possible second conquest. But he wasn't ready quite yet.

While taking my seat I made a point of letting my short black skirt ride up my long, luscious legs.

From the sudden increase in his pulse, he had not missed my performance. I made a display of crossing my legs slowly, while sitting facing him, deliberately giving him a flirtatious up the skirt glimpse of future possibilities.

He was seasoning up very nicely and, the way things were progressing, he was going to be a lovely meal.

With my leggy performance done, I responded to his inquiry of my drink preference in my sexiest voice, "Just a glass of water, please. I don't drink, not this early in the day." I then made a point of looking out onto the festive parade so he could continue enjoying the view of my legs while supposedly getting my drink of water.

When he came near with my drink of choice, I enjoyed seeing the great difficulty he was having keeping the water from spilling. I figured my meal was plenty ready for consumption. I gently pushed his arm holding the glass of water out from between us, enjoying the shocked expression that was replacing the smug look of a hunter eagerly eyeing his prey. He was stunned, frozen, while he viewed the sight of a pair of real Vampire fangs forming from my upper canine cuspids. In my mind I pictured lunging forward, locking him into place as my fangs bit deeply, oh so deeply into his throbbing neck. Before he could scream, I brought up my hand, from years of dining, and clamped off a scream that was now trapped within his lower throat.

In my orgasmic delight, I bit deeply into his throat, like the wild animal I was, and ripped out the side of his throat, spitting the mass of flesh to the carpeted floor. I greedily clamped my bloody, ravenous mouth onto his neck, sinking my hungry fangs deep into a vein. I enjoyed every morsel of his pulsating life fluids.

While the image of what could be was still alive in my mind I reached out for the glass of water with two hands so that one of my hands would brush his hand very softly, very tenderly—a promise of things to come.

With the other hand, I caught the glass as he momentarily forgot himself and almost dropped it as a result of my distracting touch. This tender moment also gave me an opportunity to enthrall him into a promise of sexual delight that got his pulse pumping so hard, I was starting to worry that he might pop something, like a vein, before I got to enjoy my properly prepared meal.

While placing the glass on the table without taking my eyes from my meal, I began moving in for my dining pleasure; he was plenty ready, but just to add a little extra spice to my meal I slowly slipped my lips up to his and gave his eagerly waiting lips a gentle kiss. I could feel him shiver with ecstasy and anticipation. Allowing my lips to glide ever so gently to his throbbing neck I lovingly eased my real fangs into this phony Vampire's neck.

He groaned peacefully into my ear, and went totally limp in my powerful arms. It was now my turn to go near orgasmic from anticipation of this so nicely seasoned meal.

With this meal's life in my hands I had to make conscious effort to remember this festive day, this day of many such meals, this day where no one had to die. Reluctantly, I drew back from my meal, allowing this phony Vampire to continue his living and his vulgar pursuit of the next woman to bed.

After cleaning up the bite wounds I placed the phony Vampire on his bed earmarked for nonsleeping, undressed him of all but his phony Vampire cape, then covered his vulgar nakedness with said cape. While enthralling him, I had emplaced the feelings within him that he had had his way with me, and it had been a mutually enjoyable experience for both partakers, in particular for him. Feeling a little sluggish from my fine dining I went back to my seat at the table and enjoyed the festivities below, temporarily enjoying the peace from above the festivities.

Later, back within the celebratory mob, as I was just taking in the sights and sounds, hands came down on my Vampire cape and a female voice from behind remarked, "You know what they say; no one knows how to do a woman better than another woman."

I turned to look into a pair of cosmetic-free eyes of a woman in yet another biker outfit. *Biker costumes must be the big thing this year.* She smelled unhealthy, even though she looked very healthy. Worried about biting someone with AIDS, I replied, "Sorry, you're not my type." I really had not heard of any Vampire being infected with AIDS, but who needs to take the chance. *AIDS was never an issue back in the old country.*

"Your loss," she called out while working back into the crowd. Not feeling any of her flippant loss, I continued my festive evening.

Later that evening, I had just walked away from a fine meal I had enjoyed—a most delicious young cowboy, really a banker in a cowboy costume—when a strong hand came down on my shoulder and with authority announced, "Excuse me."

That voice of authority sounded like a constable, if so no worries. If he saw me with the cowboy, I would just enthrall him into believing he witnessed me playing kissy face (and neck) with the cowboy, not feeding on him. I turned and found a fiftyish suit studying me. No uniform, but he still looked like a constable. He had locked his gaze on me, looking into my eyes while taking in the whole me. I decided he had to be a constable.

He continued, "I'm detective Short..."

Funny, he didn't look like a "Short" standing about six foot–seven.

"I have been watching you for some time."

Great, he witnessed me dining on the cowboy and figures he's going to perform some legalisms on me.

I was about to do my voodoo on him when he surprised me with, "I believe I know your mother."

Momentarily shocked, I stammered, "What?"

"You are the dead ringer of your mother. About twenty, yes, about twenty-three years ago I met this delightful young lady who looked just like you do today. In fact, I met her not far from here at a Halloween party. She was wearing a Vampire outfit. Well, when I saw you I was almost sure you had to be this female Vampire's, daughter. But when I saw you kissing that cowboy on the neck, just like your mother kissed me, well I just had to come up to you and introduce myself."

I gave him a good looking over and tried to picture him about twenty-some years younger, but just could not place him.

"Your name, again?" I asked him.

"Oh, we never shared names. Just tell her that her Roman Officer of old says 'hello'."

NOW I REMEMBER HIM. Yes, he was such a convincing Roman Officer. He had my mind wandering back to how it had been back in the days when Caesar just about ruled it all, and the pomp and pageant of those days.

That night, like tonight, I was in a party mood and I was going to dine often without the need to kill any of my meals. Yes, I remember that Roman Officer very well. I wondered if he would be as tasty today as he was back then?

As I mused on memories of dining on this detective, he said, "Well, I have taken up enough of your time. Enjoy the evening and remember to say 'hello' to your mother for me."

"I will, I surely will."

I walked off thinking that perhaps it's time to relocate and start over, running into old meals like that. Her thought drifted, thinking of that detective as a Roman officer, got her thinking back to how easy it had been to dine in Rome during the times of Caesar. *Rome back when it was the world's capital. The world's capital...Hmmm, maybe I should consider moving to a new world's capital, like Washington D.C. perhaps.*

Well that decision can wait another night. Tonight is for partying Vampire style, consuming to my heart's desire.

Chapter One
The Blind is Born...or is he?

Meanwhile, on the east coast a future vampire hunter is born.

I was born with very poor eyesight, but then what baby isn't?

But in my case, my eyesight was developing so slowly that when my parents took me to an eye doctor, he examined my eyes and pronounced me blind. Observing this blind child playing with his toys so close to his eyes, he sometimes bumped them into his nose. My parents took this supposedly blind child to another eye doctor who, after examining me, announced, "He does have some eyesight. His eyesight is so deteriorated that he is basically blind. He's blind and will always be blind."

Fortunately for me, my parents didn't give up that easily. When they heard of a child specialist for eye treatment, they literally went miles out of their way to have me see this doctor. He examined me and like the second doctor he announced, "He does have some eyesight," but to this he added information that the second doctor did not, "While his eyesight is developing very slowly, it is showing some signs of developing. I would like to continue seeing him, but I feel I must warn you, at some point we may have to talk eye surgery to get the job done."

Providentially for me, my eyesight continued to develop just enough to keep the surgeon's knife at bay. At three years old, I received my first pair of glasses. The lenses truly looked like they had come off the bottom of two Coke bottles, but there was an immediate effect; once they were put on me, I saw my father for the first time. He was standing, and I ran to my mother who was sitting near me and proclaimed, "Daddy big."

When it was time to go to school, the Board of Education proclaimed that I had too much eyesight to go to a school for the blind, but not enough eyesight to go to a school for the sighted. In fact, one member of the board of education went so far as to tell my father, "He'll never survive the system. Your boy will just fall through the cracks, never to graduate." My parents were fighters and, as the apple does not fall far from the tree, it turned out that I was also.

After years of being held out of school, my eyesight finally developed enough that I was visually ready to attend school for the sighted, so it was decided to put me in "Special Education" where I could learn at my own pace and feasibly enter high school somewhere near my age group...

Years later, I entered junior high just one year behind where I should have been if I had normal eyesight, but the real education fight was just beginning. The Board of Education had this rule of putting graduates of "Special Education" in lower level classes. Makes some sense when you consider the usual graduate of "Special Education" has some degree of mental challenge or as my peers would say was...A RETARD.

For the next six years, I fought the school system to get into classes I should have been in according to my mental apptitude, instead of low-level classes for the mentally- or morally-challenged student.

I had to fight this good fight on two fronts.

Front One: I had to fight to get into higher education classes that I should have been placed in instead of classes the system said I should be in, simplistic classes because I came out of "Special Education."

A perfect example was this one English class. It started with a test on Basic English structure, grammar, spelling and more. I most likely did not do as well as I could have since I was as busy trying to ignore the student beside me who was taunting me into fighting the student sitting behind me, who was just as busily banging my chair to provoke me into fighting him. Why did he want to fight me? Because it would be more interesting than taking the test.

The rest of the class was in utter mayhem, with students climbing the walls to see if they could fit into some square grooves high up the wall while other students were throwing schoolbooks out the window to watch them crash on the sidewalk below. The teacher of this class lasted a week before she needed hospital rest. (Meaning: We put her in a

9

mental hospital.) Replacing her was a series of substitutes, not any of which was stupid enough to return a second day.

One day, this little old lady walked in, who was replacing an ex-city cop from the day before, and she was fresh meat for the animals that made up the class. Eventually failing to tame the class, she just lost it. She grabbed her purse from a desk drawer, pulled out a picture, and announced, "*I am not a nobody. This is a picture of me receiving an award from the President of the United States. This award was for the Teacher of the Year.*"

A student, sitting near as he was in the first row of student desks feigning interest in the picture asked if he could see it. The little old lady in her fragile condition unthinkingly walked over and gave the famed picture to this student, saying, "Please pass it around." As I expected, he tore the picture into pieces, with the effect of tearing the little old lady to pieces at the same time. She just stood there crying before a class of laughing hyenas. I guess you can say I also lost it. From the middle of the class, I walked up to the crying mess of a little old lady, handed her purse to her and ordered, "Go see the school nurse." She took her purse and walked out. Wild animals don't like having fresh meat taken away from them, so I had no choice but to fight my way out of the classroom.

I worked my way out of a class of shouting, screaming, wild animals by shoving the closest animals off me and into school desks, adding confusion to my escape plan. Eventually, I was able to move the rumble out into the hallway where the loud-mouthed mayhem was distractingly destructive enough to send other teachers out from their classrooms.. These teachers, all men, went into crowd control mode to bring order back to their classrooms. As the animals were herded back into the classroom by four male teachers turned cattle ranchers, I started walking down the hallway, deliberately retreating from the battlefield. One teacher observing my escape called out, "Get back here or I'll send you to the principal's office."

I called back, "Don't bother, that's where I'm headed."

Without any more incidents, I marched into the principal's outer office and found his secretary with her hands full with the terrorized, screaming little old lady. The secretary looked totally out of her depth in dealing with this hysterical "teacher". It did not help that this little old lady noticeably was trying, unsuccessfully, to communicate and wail in her misery at the same time.

I ordered, "Where's Principal Jones?"

"He's in his office, there." Pointing to his closed door, totally untrained for this situation, she asked, "What happened to her?"

Ignoring the secretary's question and nearly kicking in the principal's door, I marched into Principal Jones' office and seeing him behind his desk, I angrily asked, "What the hell were you thinking sending that little old lady into that class of deranged animals?"

Ignoring my disrespectful attitude, as I was clearly in the right, he asked in a calm defeated tone, "What happened?"

"Those animals ate her alive, THAT'S WHAT HAPPENED."

"Please Jack, calm down, sit down, and tell me what happened."

I did. After giving him all the grubby details I added, "No way in hell am I going back in there. If you can't put me in another English class, I'll go to the library and teach myself." [And yes, I have had past experience teaching myself in the library because I did not belong in the class to which I was assigned, and the principal knew it. More than once the principal (here and in junior high), not having any other place to put me, put me in the library to teach myself.]

"I understand. Tomorrow I'm teaching the class..."

Interrupting him boldly, I snapped, "I don't care if you talk God himself into teaching that class, I...am...not...going...back." I emphasized each word with feeling.

He tried to stare me down, but failed. He finally said, "Right. There is another English class during this time period, but, it's an advanced class. I don't think you can handle it." I started to argue but he cut me off before I could get it out. "Also the class is full. I don't think Miss Masters will have room for you.

"SO..." I started, but again, he cut me off.

"See her after school, explain the situation, and see if she has room for you." He warned, "Don't get your hopes up as I really don't believe she has room for another student."

I visited Miss Masters, and before I could say anything, she announced, "I don't have room for you, but I will make room for you. Report here tomorrow."

I was so excited at her proclamation, that I ran out never finding out how it was she was so ready for me and so determined about finding room for me in her classroom. As for making room for me, I had to use her teacher's desk for a couple of classes until she found me a proper student desk. Once she found me a desk, she had to place it between her desk and the row of student desks nearest the window.

As to being an advanced class too difficult for me to handle, I loved that class. One assignment was to write a short story. I wrote a novelette that got me a near perfect score, the highest score she had ever given any student, though I lost points on spelling. High school students did not have computers with spell-checkers in the early 70's.

At the end of one week in a high school math class, the teacher called me up and said, "You don't belong in this class." After a dramatic pause he added, "You aced the first day exam when most of these students can't even add or subtract. Hell, some of these *high school students* didn't even spell their names correctly." He continued, "This week I have looked hard to find somewhere else to put you, but there is no other class to place you in during this time period. So I have decided to put you in my office, give you some books and let you teach yourself. When I can, I will step in and check on your progress and make myself available for any questions you may encounter. I understand you have had some experience at this self-teaching before. When feasible during the last ten minutes of each class I will give the class busy work, so I may come in and see how you are doing, answer any questions you might have and help you if you get stuck in your self education."

While the teacher tried to teach addition and subtraction to the mentally, but mostly morally challenged students, I taught myself algebra and trigonometry so well that later in college I "examed out," which meant instead of taking the required course, and then taking the final exam, I took the final exam, passed it, and was not required to take the class. I tested out with such a near perfect test score, and since I did not have to take the course, the instructor asked me if I would tutor for him, to help him with some others of his class students who needed the extra assistance. I agreed to do so.

Yes, I not only graduated from high school, but received a college degree. I should mention that, by my later college years, I needed special visual aids to get through the classes. Late in my college classes, I started taping my classes. In one class, the instructor would enter the class after the students and immediately start lecturing. For this reason, I had gotten into the routine of starting the tape player as he entered the room. One evening, he walked in and announced, "My day job is sending me to Hawaii for two weeks to fix a problem that will most likely take me two hours to fix. For the next two weeks I plan to have a real good time in Hawaii, all on a company expense account."

One of the female students asked, "Are you taking your wife and kids with you?"

Pointedly he answered, "Did you not hear me say I was going to have a good time in Hawaii? Of course I am not taking the old ball-n-chain and the rug rats with me."

The young lady sitting next to me announced, "You do realize Jack just taped all that."

If looks could kill I'd be dead right now, but the class laughed on.

Second Front: I had to fight to survive my peers. From the 50's through the 70's, "legal blindness" did not exist. You were either fully sighted, blind or A RETARDED FREAK. As previously mentioned that English class I had to fight my way out of—fighting off a whole class of students–one against dozens, Right?

Yes, Right. Part of my "Special Education." Even among the "retards" I was a freak because of my eyesight. I needed to learn to defend myself or get the crap beat out of me. You know the old trick of distracting your victim while an accomplice kneels down behind the victim. Three students tried to pull that on me once, but only once. One day on the playground, two students who were thorns in my side, walked up to me saying that they had decided to become my friends. I got suspicious. It was autumn and there were lots of dry leaves on the ground. When I heard the leaves crunching behind me, I mule kicked backward and nailed someone right in the head. I kicked him so hard that he dropped to the ground, crying. I then shoved my arms forward and rammed the other two, knocking them on their asses. No one ever tried to pull that on me a second time.

* * * *

Meanwhile in Louisiana…

Business was growing for one "lady of the night". "That prostitute in gothic-vampire outfit will give you a blow for free, well not totally free. Her price: a little bite on the neck. Hell, I don't know what's more exciting, her blow-job or her bite on the neck. Charlie swears he always comes twice- and it costs no money!"

* * * *

Meanwhile in back in Maryland…

When I was a child, my parents forced me to "go out and get fresh air." Instead of fighting to keep my bike from being stolen or dodging eggs thrown at me, I found an alternative to the tortures of my peers. Fortunately for me, next to our housing development there was a wooded area that was supposedly inhabited by the cannibalism madman called the "Rabbit Man." He was called this because his whole attire consisted of a pair of rabbit ears taken from one of the rabbits he had eaten for his dinner. He used a large bloody axe, and he always carried it with him. Oh, yes, word was that he ate kids stupid enough to enter his domain. Or desperate enough?

I spent a lot of my time in those woods. At first I was very cautious of every sound that might mean the Rabbit Man was near...

Of course, I never met up with the "Rabbit Man." When I was old enough I went from messing about in the woods to the honorable Boy Scouts. Think I made friends within such an honorable, highly moral institute as the Boy Scouts? Think again.

My patrol leader [scout assigned by the Boy Scout troop leader to be in charge of a subgroup within the troop] loved to give me every dirty duty possible, and if it was not dirty enough he would find a way to make it dirtier for the pleasure of all the others. In short, even within the Boy Scouts, I was a four-eyed retarded freak because of my low-vision. When I was old enough to progress from the Boy Scouts to the Explorers, I had no intentions of progressing on. My father and the Scoutmaster never could understand why I did not move on to the fun and adventures of The Explorers. It couldn't be because those boys that tormented me within my Boy Scout Troop were waiting for me in the Explorers, with girls to embarrass and harass me in front of no less as the

Explorers was uni-sexed. Interestingly, I was not allowed to progress within the Boy Scouts because even though I was night-blind and could not see stars, my Scoutmaster was not familiar with night blindness and refused to believe it. Meanwhile, on outings, his boys loved stealing my flashlight so they could watch me stumble around blindly in the dark.

I do recall one time when their folly of stealing my flashlight backfired on them. It was during a 50-mile hiking trip. It was such a great night that most of us guys figured it would be nicer and easier not to bother pitching tents. There was one exception; twin brothers, tenderfoots, on their first hiking trip. All day the guys had been teasing the twins to look out for bears, so when it came time to sack out for the night these two brainiacs thought they'd be smart and pitch a pup tent.

[Pup tent: Tie a rope between two trees, throw the tent canvas over the rope and secure the sides.]

The brainiacs then placed a number of rocks at both ends of the tent opening so if a bear stumbled into one side of the tent, the twins could escape from becoming the bear's dinner by exiting through the other side of the tent.

Of course, after bedding down for the night, I got the call of nature. Rooting around in my backpack, I discovered that, despite packing my flashlight at the bottom, it was gone, again. Looking around, I took notice that the Scoutmaster and the volunteer fathers were still yawning around their campfire, and I figured to use their fire to mark my way out to pee and return. After finding a nice large tree to go behind, I took care of my business. When I circled the tree to get back to my sleeping bag, I discovered that the men had sacked out for the night, putting out their campfire. I was lost.

Trying to remember my way back to my sleeping bag I found instead, yes, I found the twin's fortifications by falling over their stone guards. The twins, figuring I was a big, old hungry bear looking to eat them, ripped out the other end, yelling, "BEAR! A BEAR IS IN OUR TENT! HEELLP!" This, of course, woke everyone up, and I had lots and lots of flashlight beams to help me back to my sleeping bag.

It was during this time in my life that I made a new friend, the son of a new friend of my father, who introduced me to a fascinating magazine called, *FAMOUS MONSTERS of FILMLAND*. From the first time I eyeballed it, I instantly became a horror fan. Also during this time, my parents were having trouble finding sitters who could referee my sister and I, as we tended to fight like cats and dogs–no, really, I barked a lot at my sister, who liked to scratch at me a lot–and on and on it went. My parents found a high school sucker, Nancy. When she learned about my interest in monsters, she made a deal with me. If I did not kill or even try to kill my sister, I got to stay up past my bedtime and watch *Creature Feature* on TV with her.

For the first few times before Count Gore DeVol started to host the night's Creature Feature, Nancy made a point of telling me, "Now remember, what you see is only make-believe, there is nothing really scary about these movies. Certainly nothing that can hurt you."

I took her instruction so much to heart that years later while sneaking off to view Hammer Horror movies with two of my buds, as they totally freaked out during the movies, I, Mr. Cool, would prevail. Nothing scares *the Man*.

Who could not watch those great Hammer Horror movies and not become a great fan of Vampires? From Christopher Lee's Dracula to all those sexy female Vamps.

One more note on my sister. Even though we fought like cats and dogs when we were younger, when we matured, we developed a pact. If some girl gave my sister a hard time it was her problem; if some guy gave her a hard time, it was my problem. My sister's first job was at our local Roy Rogers Restaurant. There was a young man who liked to talk dirty to the girls, this included my sister. When she told me how upsetting it was, I visited this Roy Rogers, and I made a point of arriving when they were not busy. When I walked in, I looked around. The place wasn't quiet, it was dead. The only people I could find were two serving girls standing behind the counter, eagerly waiting for me to walk the snake and upon arriving in front of the register, give my order. Instead, I walked around to the side of the snake, came up beside the register and asked one of the serving girls to ask "Charlie" to come out to see me. She complied by disappearing into the back. The girl returned from the back and told me, "Charlie says he's too busy right now."

Loudly, I proclaimed, "Well, tell *Charlie* that if he does not get his ass out here right now I will go back there to see him, and he will not be happy."

No sooner than that was said then some big guy was standing behind the counter-girl apologizing profusely. I can't imagine Charlie knew what he was apologizing for, but he was very enthusiastically doing so.

Finding ourselves between the end of the front counter and right next to some bar seats where a diner could sit and look out into the parking lot, I introduced myself as Erica's brother and invited him to be seated; he sat. Taking the bar stool next to him I began giving him a verbal lesson in manners his parents should have given him, on how men should treat women as ladies. I'm not saying women are second-rate citizens, I just believe woman should be treated like ladies not like hookers. He seemed to hang on every word. I finished my lecture by saying, "If my sister should tell me you require a second, more physical lesson on the subject, I will be back."

At this point, I noticed that the two serving girls where wiping down the cash register so as to be in easy eavesdropping distance, so I added, a little louder for their benefit, "In fact, if my sister tells me you're still having trouble behaving around any of the girls here, I will be back for that second lesson."

He assured me that would not be necessary, and it wasn't. There was an interesting development to this. In the future when I walked in and ordered and paid for a small drink, I'd receive a tray with a large drink, large fries and a roast beef and possibly even a hamburger. While this was really cool, I was a little worried that this gratitude from the girls might get them into trouble, since they were handing out free food. I told my sister that, while I was enjoying the free food, I did not want the girls getting in trouble for it. She informed me that the female manager was very aware of the "Charlie" problem, but was at a loss to figure out how to handle it. She was *very* appreciative of my handling the problem for her. The free meals were her request. They were orders the girls enjoyed fulfilling.

Growing up, I developed an old-fashioned attitude toward women and a man's treatment of a woman. In my first year of junior high school, apparently there were enough of us students coming out of "special education" that some county school brain thought it was a good idea to combine all of us into our own special class of retards. This class consisted of mental misfits like Jack who did not talk much, but if asked a direct question would answer by clucking like a chicken, or Betty who didn't know much, except that she was easy on the eyes. She spent a lot of time messing with her hair and her clothes. Then there were the mental delinquents like the James Gang (as in Jesse James gang). This "gang" consisted of Jose, who was mostly mouth, and James who could protect Jose from his big mouth. Then there were students like myself, who had come through the "special education" program as a way of making up school years due to health or a physical handicap.

One day, the teacher, who looked as if she were young enough to have come right out of college, could not find the book of poems from which she had planned to read. With the school library right outside the door, she decided she would trust the class to behave long enough to get another copy of the book. This lack of judgment just shows that she probably was just out of college and this was her first class.

After she left the room, one of the guys proudly showed off his possession of the missing book. While making a big deal of putting the book back from where he temporarily stole it, Jose (a real moral degenerate with a big mouth) commented to Betty, a real shapely, blue-eyed blond, how nice her outfit looked. He finished his discourse with on her attire, "but it would look even nicer on the empty chair beside you."

Betty responded, "Like you'll ever see that."

"Bet you I will," Jose retorted. He then got out of his chair and made a big deal about walking up to Betty, who was not very bright. She supported her challenge by getting out of her chair to face off Jose.

Betty was wearing a white blouse with a dark blue vest that matched her skirt. Once in front of her, he started making a big production of unbuttoning her vest.

Betty just stood there, looking incredulous, and the class looked on.

After Jose had Betty's vest unbuttoned, in show-off fashion, he flicked the vest off her shoulders, and it fell to the floor.

The class looked on, in silence.

As Betty just stood looking shocked, Jose this *rape* was going too far, and **I** started looking for the return of the teacher, meanwhile Jose continued unbuttoning Betty's blouse. Betty, like a deer in headlights, just stood there looking shocked, and the class just looked on.

When Jose had her blouse more than half-unbuttoned, and Betty's white bra was making an appearance, things, in my opinion, had gone too far.

As the class just looked on, I looked toward the doorway for the expected re-appearance of the teacher. Since her re-appearance was not yet forthcoming, I made my move.

I charged out of my seat, rushed up beside Jose and, feeling full of moral fortitude, grabbed a handful of the back of his shirt and pulled him off Betty. With rapist and victim separated, I stepped in between them. While I just stood there quietly daring Jose to make a move, Betty stood behind me, just crying.

Three girls jumped into action. While two of them got Betty back into her seat, the third grabbed up Betty's vest and the three girls went about redressing Betty while trying to calm her down. They were failing. As Betty continued crying, the girls got her clothes back on her. Meanwhile I just stood there feeling full of holy righteousness, waiting for Jose to make the wrong move, any move, and they would be cleaning him off the walls and ceiling.

The very mouthy Jose just stood there staring back at me, too wary to even say a word. I guess he was not totally stupid (just sounded totally stupid a lot).

The teacher finally walked in and ordered, "To your seats, everyone."

As "everyone" obeyed, she marched back behind her desk, slammed the book in her hand down onto the prodigal book and announced in her best demigod voice, "Nothing happened. I was not here so nothing happened," and that was the last of that—I wish. (But that's another story.)

While in high school, I had one girlfriend that lasted one date. Christina and I not only went to the same high school, but also attended the same church. I turned a youth church outing into a date for the two of us. First, we went with the group to a Rock-n-Roll Christian band concert, and then we ordered pizza at the neighborhood Pizza Pub.

After placing our order at the register and getting our dinner number, Christina followed my lead to separate from the rest of the group for our date. It was just my luck that two young under-aged drunks took a shine to Christina and followed us. After we found a seat and the drunks tried to join us, I politely asked the two to leave, "We like it right here, don't we Bill?"

So we tried to move back within the safety of the group with whom we had arrived, but there were no seats anywhere near them, so we sat where we could, and the drunks followed.

At a new table, I sat down across from my lovely date to enjoy her beauty and the two drunks moved in, one standing on either side of her. The mouthier of the two set his pitcher of beer and his mug down on the table between us. Following this, he placed his mouth close to Christina's ear and, between her eyes widening and his hand holding his crotch, I could guess what he asked her.

In one fluid movement, I shot out of my seat and planted an uppercut that sent the mouthy drunk backward so hard that he landed on top of some family's dinner, on their table. I quickly picked up the half-empty pitcher of beer and flung the contents at Bill the Drunk. I then changed the position of the now empty pitcher of beer so that the side of the pitcher could rudely smack Bill the Drunk up-side his face. I stopped when his hands, one with his beer in it, went up in the universal sign of surrender.

This conflict brought every male employee in the pub into action. The one I assumed to be the manager ordered some of his employees to throw the drunks out, and then he turned to us. "What happened here?" he demanded.

I told him and while doing so, I observed and overheard what was most likely the assistant manager apologizing to the family for the drunk falling onto their table. He assured them that they would receive a new pizza, without a drunk topping. When I finished telling the manager what happened, he got huffy and ordered, "Finish your meal and leave."

"I beg your pardon." Now it was my turn to get huffy. "Who do you think you're talking to? We were just unpleasantly confronted by two under-aged drunks in *your* establishment. Tell me, *sir*, who sold them their beers? You or I? Who do you think you're giving attitude to?"

20

Looking a bit shocked, he just walked away. Coming home on her first date, smelling of beer that had splashed off Bill the Drunk might have had something to do with Christina's parents deciding she was too young for dating and would not be dating again until after she finished high school.

I did not date much in high school. It is hard to develop self-confidence when you have a large number of young gorillas on your back on a daily basis. These young gorillas also hung out around town, not just in school. Later, when these same young gorillas got car keys and I, the vision freak, still used a bicycle, well I just cannot tell you how many times a car full of laughing young gorillas drove me off the road, to their highly vocal, humiliating, delight. These young gorillas usually got their way because we were on school grounds and they were always in numbers. I had to be a "good boy."

Years later, I discovered traveling by Metro bus. During a trip back from visiting the National Zoo, as we neared the Maryland/D.C. line, the bus was so full that people were already standing. I was sitting near the front so I could keep track of the bus's progress within the abilities of my weakened eyesight.

At one stop a very pregnant woman who looked ready to pop got on the bus. Being taught to be a gentleman, I asked the woman, "Would you like to sit?"

As I got up, a punk whom I had not noticed standing by, jumped into my vacated seat before the pregnant woman could sit down. I heard him move into my seat more than I saw him. When I looked at him, he smiled like the Cheshire cat, and thought he was sooo cool.

I reached down, grabbed his vest, and in one move yanked him back onto his feet, standing next to me. As I stared at him, daring him to make the wrong move, I said to the pregnant woman, "Would you like to sit down now?" I heard her sink down to the seat as I continued to stare this jerk down. He just melted within my glare like butter on a hot frying pan. Within the tight environment of a public bus, where riders mostly just mind their own business, the strangest thing I have ever witnessed as a rider occurred. About half or more of the riders applauded their approval of what had just taken place. As we came up to the next stop, the punk still under my glare said very politely, "This is my stop. May I get past you?" I stepped to the side. As the punk carefully moved past me, I overheard a woman say, "That's not his stop. He never gets off anywhere near here."

As the bus continued, I felt a light tug on my pants, and looked down to see the pregnant woman wanting my attention. "I really needed to sit down and get off my sore feet. I must have done too much today." With real feeling she added, "Thank you so much."

Addressing the pregnant lady, I replied, "No problem, ma'am."

During my junior high and high school years, I was seeing a low vision specialist. It was during these years that I started reporting a growing difficulty seeing moving objects like basketballs, volleyballs, and footballs. The specialist just put it off as oversized blind spots. Don't get me started on my "oversized blind spots" and my physical education classes during these years. You think guys can be cruel. I still have nightmares of my boy/girl volleyball games in PE.

I graduated in 1974, while the very unpopular Vietnam War was still underway, and so was the draft. My mother took me to the local draft office, where they looked at my medical records, particularly my eye doctor's reports and without even giving me a physical exam or another additional thought, they handed me my "4-F" draft card and went on to the next person. [4-F classification. unfit for military service]

My mother was so happy that her boy could not be drafted and forced to possibly die for his county that she wanted to go out and celebrate. She could not understand why I did not feel the same. Puzzled by my lack of joy, she said, "Honey, don't you understand? You can't be drafted. You don't have to worry about possibly going to fight a war where you could get hurt, or worse. So why are you looking so down?"

"All my life my peers have been telling me what a retarded freak I am. Now I have an official card from the government, making it official. I AM A FREAK." For my mother's sake I left out the word 'fucking' that my peers usually had preceding "freak." Being a card carrying four-eyed freak was not sitting well with me.

Two years after I graduated from high school, the low vision specialist discovered his error in calling my eye problem "oversized blind spots" and sent me to Johns Hopkins for verification. There I spent a long day of eye tests. Some were so painful that (some years later) when they tested my family, my father was amazed that I kept coming back, and my sister passed out during her testing.

At the end of my first day of hard testing, my mother and I ended the day in the head researcher's office, where the eye specialist looked me over and turned to my mother and announced, "Your son has RP. He is going blind, and it's all *your fault*."

Chapter Two
Going Blind

After a dramatic pause, he continued, "Your son is going blind from Retinitis Pigmentosa or RP. He has black spots or pigmentation forming in the back of his eyes. Eventually the pigmentation will cause all the rods and cones to die, and at that point your son will be totally blind. At this point we don't know much about RP, except that it is highly hereditary only through the woman's side, so he must have gotten his RP from you."

My mother was no fool and she kept her cool, until we got out into the parking lot. Once we were in the car, she put the key into the ignition and sat back. For the first and only time in my life, I witnessed my mother cry. She had just been told her son is going blind and it was all her fault. Can you blame her?

Retinitis Pigmentosa

In the 70's when I was first diagnosed with RP only two basic facts were known. The first fact was that RP formed dark spots or pigments in the back tissue of the eye (the retinas). Hence the name Retinitis Pigmentosa (Latin for pigmentation of the retinas). How clever. The second fact was that RP ran rampant through the family and was carried only by the females of the family.

Those basic facts were only half-right.

Years later, after many scientific studies and the various RP studies using computers to correlate the data, it was discovered that while many victims of RP had it running strongly through the family, there were many (like me) with no one else losing their sight to RP. Possibly a nonhereditary strain? This brought about theories and conjectures that there are possibly two or more types of RP.

Symptoms.

Night blindness. The inability to see in dim light situations. Night blindness is the earliest sign of RP. [Being night blind does not necessarily mean you have RP. You can be night blind and not have RP.] In my case I was always night blind.

Loss of peripheral vision: Your peripheral vision is your side vision, that vision not in the direct line of sight. In my case, I started noticing a real problem in junior high and high school sports. Large objects like volleyballs and basketballs would disappear from sight before getting to me. At the time, my low vision doctor assumed that it was oversized blind spots, since little was known about RP. Blind spots are areas of the peripheral vision where we don't have vision. Everyone has a small blind spot in each eye where the nerves go out to the brain. Eventually my low vision specialist could see the pigmentations causing these "oversized blind spots" as he had been calling them for years.

Tunnel vision: Loss of the peripheral vision causes a tunnel vision effect with the remaining sighted area getting smaller and smaller.

True tunnel vision: With only the use of the central vision and no peripheral vision, someone with RP as if they were looking through a paper towel roll.

Tunnel vision with only light perception in the peripheral vision: the loss of sight is not as bluntly noticeable as in true tunnel vision, but just as visually daunting. I eventually had to start using a white cane because of the combination of tunnel vision and lazy eye muscles, making it impossible to see moving objects or to see while I am moving.

Reverse tunnel vision: The central vision is attacked before the peripheral vision causing the victim to be able to see only with their side vision. While in various RP studies I have met a number of folks with this visual problem.

Vision loss: The end result is total blindness due to loss of all the rods and cones in the retinas.

Treatment: Supplements of Vitamin A and Lutein.

Retina transplants: Various studies are underway that may lead to the replacement of the damaged rods and cones or by implant of a computer chip. The chip would replace the damaged cells.

I was in a study group which was testing the use of virtual glasses. They were hoping that the glasses, worn by a victim of RP, could fool the brain into seeing normally by getting an image to the brain and bypassing the damaged areas of the retinas. The study ended due to funding issues, but was picked up by a computer gaming company to make virtual glasses for computer gamers.

This unpleasant first visit to the Wilmer Eye Institute at Johns Hopkins was the beginning of many years of unpleasant testing. I should mention that this point that while many of the tests were bothersome to downright painful, the staff at Johns Hopkins was very pleasant throughout—with one exception, the initial diagnosis incident given to my mother.

The easiest tests were of the normal variety, designed to test the decline in your eyesight. One was the normal peripheral eye test where they stick your head into a large cone and have you indicate when the dot is visible and when it goes missing. I took this test for so many years that the testing went from a manual recording, to the system being totally computerized. Personally, as a programmer, I felt more comfortable with the computer results being more accurate.

The night vision testing was very unpleasant. The first stage of the testing was putting test subjects in a totally dark room for hours. Happily for us test subjects, the test administrators quickly learned it was wise to put more than one person at a time in the room so the test subjects could pass the time conversationally with each other. When they tested my family, it was early in the studies. My sister was put in a room by herself, where she panicked and fainted during this phase of testing. Ever heard of sensory deprivation? [Sensory deprivation. Short-term sessions of sensory deprivation are described as relaxing and conducive to meditation; however, extended or forced sensory deprivation can result in extreme anxiety, hallucinations, bizarre thoughts and depression.]

My personal favorite for pure pain was when they put my chin in a chin vise, put a flash camera in front of my eyes, and took a dozen or more flash photos of each eye. I found this particularly interesting considering one of the first things they tell you early on with RP is to avoid bright light, as it could aggravate the RP into developing faster. I don't know if this testing aggravated the RP, but it sure aggravated me. Not to mention the pain. This diagnoses of pending blindness occurred during my college years.

During all these years of testing, life went on.

After high school, I moved on to college. My major studies in the field of Wildlife Biology. My future plan was to get a career where I could spend lots of time in the woods alone meanwhile making a living. After all, I had lots of experience spending time in the woods alone while hiding from my peers "getting fresh air" as a kid.

Classes were going great for about two years, when our college program got a new department head. Mrs. March tried to pull some fancy reprogramming that resulted in some of us students getting burned. This gave me time to reevaluate my situation: With the strong potential prospect of going blind, I suspended my studies. I did not see much of a career as a blind wildlife biologist.

Nailing a library clerk job with a major corporation, I started taking internal classes in computer science and found I had a real future and enjoyment in that direction. When I found out the corporation would pay for my evening college classes, I went back to college to become a full programmer. When I progressed from library clerk to assistant programmer within the corporation, I found a real first-rate apartment only a few blocks from work.

About five years later, just like any weekday morning, I set off to walk to work. On the way to work, I seemingly bounced off a sidewalk sign and a pole along the way. When I walked into my office, I accidently kicked a trash can across the room, a trash can the cleaning crew had failed to properly put back after emptying. Something was really wrong.

After work, it was bowling night. When I left work, I took the bus downtown to the bowling alley. When I got off the bus at my usual bus stop, I turned and bounced nose-first off a telephone pole. There was no doubt about it, I had lost considerable eyesight overnight. This was a possible occurrence I had been warned about often during my RP testing visits.

I had been educated in the possibility that with RP one could have a sudden noticeable loss of eyesight, and literally overnight this had happened to me. This was not all bad. This event was not severe enough to have left me fully blind—this time.

The very next day I went into the Employee Assistance department and explained what had happened. I explained that I had gone from slightly legally blind to very legally blind, and for starters I needed mobility training.

The next day I was called back to Employee Assistance department and was introduced to Miss May from the Maryland Department of Rehabilitation.

When I was asked my goals, I replied, "I'm currently in college, taking night classes, studying to be a programmer."

"Computers. That's a great field for the blind. There is so much technology out there to assist the blind, or legally blind in the performance of their work."

Interest peaked, "Really, like what?"

"There are CCTVs (Closed Circuit Television Viewers), a magnifier that can blow up a whole page onto a TV screen. There are voice and Braille computers; and voice readers like the Kurzweil Reader...."

After some discussion on the various machines for the handicapped she said, "Don't worry I will set you up. But for now, I need to set you up with some white cane training."

"White cane?"

"A visual aid that will assist you in getting around safely; as well as let others around you know that you are visually impaired and may not be able to see them."

Later that day I got a phone call from a Miss Becker, a mobility instructor, who set up an appointment to see me at work the very next day. She continued to see me at work and around about the work complex until I had my white cane mobility training down properly using the fiber straight cane she had provided at no cost. On the cane was the writing "NFB" so I asked, "What is this NFB?"

"The National Federation of the Blind is an organization about and for the blind. I highly recommend you get in touch with them. They can be very helpful for the blind in many ways."

She also educated me in the various types of white canes, "This is a straight cane. There are also folding and collapsible white canes. The collapsible canes collapse up into itself when not in use. I have been told that the problem with the collapsible cane is that it may collapse while in use, so I recommend the folding white cane. It is in four to five parts with a large flexible band running down the center. When not in use you fold it up and loop the end of the band around the cane. When not in use it can then fit in your pocket."

She must have called the NFB and gave them my number, as I got a call from a local member to invite me to their next meeting. The conversation ended with me agreeing that I would attend their next meeting.

There was this one interesting, not to mention a bit surprising incident. Walking into a Peoples Drug Store I bumped into a big man who tried to walk into the store at the same time.

"Sorry," I said quickly.

"On no, I'm sorry. It was all my fault," this big man exclaimed with strong feeling.

I just stood there, possibly with my mouth open. I was surprised when I realized this was the same man I had bumped into in just the same way a week earlier. This same big man who, after I apologized for accidently bumping him, angrily threatened to tear my head off for being so rude and clumsy as to get in his way. The difference, a week ago I did not have my white cane with me.

I attended my first NFB meeting. As one going blind, the first thing that impressed me was how many professionally employed members were in attendance. There were programmers, systems analysts (which I had some great conversations with on programming and special equipment in the field of program design), a lawyer, small company owners, and several members who worked in fields related to the blind such as Braille proofreaders who worked in and for the government. I was quickly impressed that there were real blind people in real professional careers. It gave me hope for that day if or when I went totally blind.

During my first meeting, I also learned about a couple of great sources for supplies and adaptive education; Volunteers for the Visually

Handicapped (VVH) and The Lighthouse for The Blind. A couple of classes at the Lighthouse in cooking taught me that I was a real disaster in the kitchen. My gastronomy specialty remained F-or-F. *Fast* (food) *or Frozen* (microwave (nuked) dinners). There was a pizza place right on the way home from work that normally you would walk into, cross the tables area, and place your order at the counter. I visited the restaurant so often, ordering the same type pizza, that eventually all I had to do was walk in and sit down. They would bring me out my Coke and when my pizza was ready (the same pizza I always ordered) they would bring it out as well. I did not need to place a dinner order. I just paid at the table.

Both VVH and Lighthouse had social group activities. For instance, with the VVH group, we went to the C&O canal for tandem biking with plenty of sighted volunteers. I brought a date to this one, a young lady I had met at church. We learned that tandem biking wasn't for us. For one thing, it just did not seem to work with a little lightweight in the front and a big old blind guy in the back seat. Second, yes, we did try biking with the blind guy up front. This got rid of the weight distribution problem, but can you guess what the new problem was?

The Lighthouse had a yearly tradition I always looked forward to—a trip to the Baltimore stadium to see my Orioles *play ball*. One year, the fans were really giving the umpire a hard time. I got an idea, which I was a little late acting on. Just as everyone stopped yelling at the umpire, I raised my folding white cane in the air and yelled, "Give that umpire my white cane." He had been ignoring everyone else, but he just had to turn to see me waving my white cane at him and yelling again, "Give that umpire my white cane." If you're wondering, no, I had not had a few beers by then, I had just gotten into the spirit of the mob that day. I started a new tradition that lasted years. The group, often many of the same people from year to year, playfully teased me about giving the umpire my white cane. One year I was ready for them; I had brought two white canes with me. Just in case the umpire needed one.

During my interview with Employee Assistance, I mentioned that the sudden loss could happen again and leave me totally blind at any time. I might have mentioned that it would be great if I got my programming degree and got into a programming department before I went totally blind, so I had some visual experience within my chosen career. They acted on this.

A week later Employee Assistance called me in and introduced me to Mrs. Walker, Head of Internal Programming Department. The result was that I was offered and accepted a programming position before I finished my education and received my degree, "..so you will have the optimal time to develop program experience while your eyesight lasts."

This was great. But what about those visual devices to aid me in my work? Calls to my rehab counselor all were the same, "Lack of funding, complain to your local Congressman."

Following such a call, I received another call from my mother, who could hear the disappointment in my voice from my talk with my rehab counselor. After asking about my "moody mod", she asked for my counselor's name and phone number.

The next day, my rehab counselor called me at my apartment because I had been up all night with a migraine headache and had called in sick to get some sleep. She set up an appointment at my apartment for that very afternoon to discuss my needs and to give me a required IQ test. Before the meeting, I called my mother who informed me that when the counselor gave her the "Lack of funding, complain to your local Congressman." My mother responded with, "I work with Congressman so-n-so, Congressman so-n-so and Congressman so-n-so. Which one would you like me to *have call you?*"

During the IQ test, Miss May made the observation that I would make a great programmer because I think like a computer. During one part of the test, the person tested is supposed to look at a circle and check the chart to see what the number for that circle is (for example "1"), record it under the circle, go to the next figure (for example, a square), check the chart to see that the number for squares are (say "2"), go to the next (for example, another circle), check the chart to see what the number is and so on..

I looked at the circle, checked the chart and put a "1" under all the circles, checked the chart for squares and put a "2" under all the squares and checked the chart for triangles and put a "3" under all the triangles and so on. Miss May commented that my system was the fastest she had

31

ever seen, I had handled it like a computer would have. I should make a great programmer.

This was the early 80's. Computer-wise, this was still the time of mainframe computing. There was no such thing as PCs. Dumb terminals connected a human to one very big computer and that was all the terminal could perform. All the real work was done at the mainframe computer, hence the term "Dumb Terminal."

The Corporation, note the corporation, not Maryland Rehab., got me the first talking terminal on the East coast, so of course they also got me a news reporter to report the event. The interview went well—almost. I thought the reporter had left, so I was quite surprised when a question my boss asked just after the interview was printed in the article...

My hearing impaired boss asked, "Does this terminal have both voice input and output?"

Having a little fun with the women programmers within our department, I pointed at the large speaker under the CRT screen and answered, "No. It's like a woman, all mouth—no ears."

Later, when the article was printed, my girlfriend read it to me, rolled up the newspaper, and hit me over the head with it. I will not tell you what my mother had to say when she read the article, but no, she did not cry.

A teacher of the blind after reading the article called me for permission to bring her students out to see my equipment and to allow her blind students a chance to talk with a visually handicapped professional. I told her it was fine with me, but she most likely would have to talk to Employee Services (previously known as Employee Assistance Dept. through corporate restructuring) either for permission or to be referred to the right people to give her such permission. The next day she called again. She had received permission and wanted to set up a day and time that was good for me. After all the details of the visit were accomplished, she added, "I have a new student, who just lost her eyesight as a result of a drunk driver. She sees no future ahead of her without sight. Her name is Mary. Could you possibly spend a little time with her?"

"Sure. No problem."

The teacher and her young class of blind students arrived and for the most part showed great interested in the equipment and what I had to say about working, even though I had very poor eyesight. There was this one little girl who was a noticeable recluse. Remembering what the teacher had said about a particular little newly blind girl named Mary, I touched her shoulder and asked, "What is your name?"

Shyly she answered, "Mary."

Setting the terminal controls to read what I typed, I typed and the computer said, "Hi, Mary. I'm the computer talking to you."

That put some life into her.

The entire office got quite a laugh when after the students had left, and after they had had a real good look at the terminal, blind style. The boss got out some cleanser to clean off all the many little fingerprints to be found all over the computer.

Later I got a call from the teacher of the blind students. "I just wanted to thank you for your time. The kids were fascinated by the whole visit. By the way, Mary has gotten into the program, she says 'So I can be a programmer like Mr. Poisner and his talking computer.'"

With the realization that this Christmas might be the last Christmas I could enjoy *seeing* Christmas lights I developed a new admiration for all the many Christmas illuminations and the many fancy lit displays of Christmas.

Eventually I finished school, got my degree and became a full programmer. With the increase in pay, I moved to a larger apartment, which was even closer to work. After I moved in, I discovered one major problem. I now had to cross two major highways to get to work. My biggest problem was crossing George Ave. and living long enough to get to the other side. As trained, I would listen to the traffic pattern and when the parallel traffic moved, I would point my white cane out and move into the crosswalk—where more often than not an impatient driver would violate my right to the crosswalk and cut me off. Sometimes they would get so close as to hit my white cane. Sometimes they would get so close as to smack my white cane right out of my hand.

One morning, such a driver smacked my white cane clean out of my hand. I heard his car brake and thought, *well, at least this driver is going to be nice enough to help me find my white cane.* Instead, this male driver got out of his car and yelled angrily, "You just hit my brand new car with your stick!"

I called back, "No sir, you just smacked my white cane with your car, while violating my right to this crosswalk. You do know what a crosswalk is, don't you?" Changing my tone gradually with each word from nice to angry, I requested, "Sir, would you mind helping me find my white cane so I can wrap it around your neck?" He just got back into his new car and sped off. Someone else helped me find my now "L-shaped" folding white cane. My cane was bent so badly I had to feel my way back to my apartment and get out my fiberglass straight cane, my backup cane.

One morning my boss and I got inundated with phone calls from customers, work-related friends, etc. All of them wanted to know if I was alright. Seems a local radio station reported, "A blind man was killed last night crossing George Ave." I later found out the blind man was a fellow member of my Chapter of the NFB and a friend.

Later it got out that he was killed by a drunk driver who was racing another car, and that the police did nothing about it, because the victim's dog guide had him outside the crosswalk, despite the fact that the victim and his dog were next to the crosswalk.

From that incident, the NFB got busy and prevailed in getting a law passed that basically says, "As neither a white cane nor a dog guide can differentiate the white lines of a crosswalk, if a visually handicapped individual is adjacent to a crosswalk, legally it is the same as if the visually handicapped individual is in the crosswalk."

Chapter Three
Going, Going, Gone

Meanwhile in Louisiana…

Sitting behind her plush desk within her luxurious office with a diffident French feel to it, her current endeavors in business accounting were rudely interrupted by the often hot-blooded Hank crashing into the room. He was her driver and her only employee (not including his temporary replacement while Hank was out sick).

"Hank, you're looking much better, but what's with the gold chain and cross? Your latest attack of Swamp Fever give you religion?"

"You could say that, demon bitch."

Confused by his rude mood, and using her heightened vampire senses, she could quickly evaluate that her single employee was not under any mental confusion brought on from any medical fever—his body temperature was around normal. It was quite obvious that his anger was very real. She could sense it from his elevated heartbeat. He smelled temptingly of fear, and it was truly making her hungry. Making an effort to keep her calm, she asked, "Hank, I don't know what crawled up your butt hole, but I strongly suggest you calm down."

In a voice still reeking of anger, Hank replied, "Remember when you stole me from Jo-Jo, to be your driver? Remember how I said it was 'fate' that you chose me?"

"Yes, but…"

Deliberately interrupting his lady boss, a first ever…

Rosy couldn't help the distracting thought, *He really does have a head of steam on.*

Taking no notice of his boss's momentary distracted thoughts, he went on, "When I was just a tadpole living with my parents, and while I was very sick with the swamp fever, someone…or something visited my parent's bed-n-breakfast back in the bayou. Up in my room, in the loft of the house, I could not see this new visitor, but I could hear its distinctive voice, a very horrifying voice that could only come *from a creature of hell.* I also heard, and to this day can still hear, that demon kill both of my parents. That demon or vampire, afterward, bled both my parents dry, then left me still alive."

Hank continued, with fevered hatred, "Last week when the swamp fever took me again, I heard that demonic voice, yet again—
your voice, your true voice." He removed a wooden stake from behind his back, where she knew he usually carried a pistol, for protection. With a stake displayed in his hand, her only employee continued, "It was fate that brought us together, and fate has brought me to the very monster that killed my parents, to the monster who bled my parents dry, to the monster I gave an oath to kill someday. If I should fail this night, I have sent off a message to my kin, telling them that you are my parent's killer. If I should fail this night, they will come after you to grant my parents their due rest."

With the memory of how she used to visit the bayou from time-to-time for the thrill of the hunt and the crimson meal, she decided she had heard enough. With blinding speed, truly supernatural, she hurdled over her desk (sending her forgotten accounting paperwork flying in all directions), and planted herself in front of her soon-to-be ex-employee.

Hank suddenly felt a vise grip clamp on his throat and another on his wrist. The grip on his wrist crushed bones, causing searing pain, and he dropped the weapon to the floor, where it rolled harmlessly away from the fray, as if it did not want to be around to see what horror would follow. Hank's shocked mind tried to process, through the pain, the fanged revulsion in his eyesight. This fanged creature of disgust still had some disturbing resemblance to what had been his most lovely boss.

Unable to move his head due to the vise grip on his neck, Hank's bulging eyes moved to his hand, which no longer held a weapon. When his boss released her grip on his crushed wrist, his eyes bulged even more at the sight and the pain of his limp hand falling forward. He would have screamed at either the sight or the pain of the involuntary movement, but the scream was still being choked off by the vise-like grip still around his neck. The grip was so tight that his shocked mind had not yet registered the lack of life preserving air, like he was going to live long enough to worry about a lack of air.

A demonic voice ordered, "Hank," in a command voice that was not to be ignored. Hank turned his gaze back to the demonic version of his once beautiful boss. She (it?) continued, "Hank, crosses only affect vampires with a guilty conscience; I have no such weaknesses. I'd have you for dinner, but I don't want to take a chance at receiving your swamp fever. It really is a shame you had to lose your head. But, wait, you haven't totally lost your head." With a laugh Hank hadn't heard since the feverish night his parents were both killed, Rosy brought her other hand up to Hank's neck. She unscrewed his head until it popped off like a bottle cork releasing a spray of blood, like crimson champagne bubbly, a bubbly she would have gladly sunk her demonic lips over, but even a demon does not want to battle with swamp fever.

Changing back to her mortal appearance, she laughed again at her little jokeas she tossed her ex-employee away, just as if his limp hundred-something pound body was nothing but an oversized rag doll. Hank's version of champagne had made quite a mess of the rich office interior, but that really was no concern for Rosy. Rosy Báthory was busy giving real consideration to her ex-employee's unintended warning of the possibilities of additional foes ["kin"]. *It's time to move on. Lady, it's not like you have not performed this dance before.*

When her headless, expired driver crashed backward into a wall, only to slide to the floor, his forgotten head rolled away. She was already making plans to gather up her liquid assets, her package of new identities (including new names). She was going to have to get her clothes together and decide how she was going to travel and to where?

Where, indeed. Ever since her encounter with that constable during a Mardi Gras a couple of years ago, the one who reminded her of fun-filled days of frolicking in ancient Rome, then the capital of the world, there was the consuming of all those hated Christians and political prisoners.

This was surely a lot more fun than being cooped up in a dingy, old castle watching age steal her beauty from her. *When you think about it, it's no wonder I went a little crazy bathing and consuming all that handmaiden blood.*

She returned to the idea of relocating to the current capital of the world–Washington, D.C. *But before I go east, I think I will go west to spend some time enjoying the sights, sounds and blood of Vegas.*

Meanwhile, in Maryland....

Testing at Johns Hopkins continued. The results showed that my peripheral vision was continuing to decline at a slow rate, but my central vision was hanging in well. Looking over my history, the research doctor added, "I see you had a sudden, overnight spurt of activity of RP development. Just a reminder, the next time that happens you could go to sleep sighted and wake up totally blind, permanently blind."

Meanwhile my ride to church disappeared, a young man who was having marital problems to the point that his wife walked out on him. He could not take the stress of his impending divorce and had to be hospitalized, I was told, for an extended time.

I needed a new ride, so I called my sister. She had recently moved into her first apartment and it was close by. "Sure, I'd be glad to give you a ride to church, but you do realize I don't attend Monrosa. (*Well, that explains why I haven't seen her at church lately.*) I have been going to a closer church, a little church called Banner Church of Christ."

"And what is a Church of Christ?"

"Basically it's like a Baptist church, but a bit more liberal. They have a singles social group you will enjoy," she ended in a playful tone.

"I'm sold." Matching her playful tone, I continued, "So what time should I be ready to be picked up?"

"Sunday school class starts at 10 a.m. It's nice to get there early and spend some social time before class begins. So let's say about 9:15, OK? That will get us to church about a half-hour before class starts, plenty of time to socialize."

Before the class started, Erica introduced me to some of the members of the class and the church singles program, both male and female. My first impression was that of a real fun and friendly group.

The class started with announcements including, "Just a reminder. After services there is a get-together at Taco Taco."

After class, I asked Erica, "So what is Taco Taco?"

"It's a new Mex-restaurant that is fancier than a fast food place, but not too expensive. I hear it's really nice. Don't worry. I'll drive you there; just meet me back at the car after the service. I did not think to mention it, but I will not be sitting with you during the service."

"Oh', already ashamed to be seen with your big brother?" I joked.

"That and I'll be sitting up with the choir, singing," she answered playfully.

The service was impressive. The choir was inspiringly good for a small church singing group. Reverend Bob was very moving with his sermon on how little sins can slip you in to a life of greater sins.

After the service, I was a bit delayed getting back to Erica's car as I was extremely welcomed by many of the church-goers. It did not take long to see this was a very friendly church group. Erica was waiting for me, very understanding of my delay.

At Taco Taco we got separated and I found myself at a table of near total strangers, I say "near" as I had met and talked earlier with Jasmine and Tom. There were three others at our table whom I had not met, including a lovely little thing that was sitting right across from me. I quickly got to know this Dolly Parton double as Diana.

When things started coming to an end, my sister appeared from nowhere. "So you ready to leave?" I wasn't quite sure how to answer that, when Diana answered for me, "I'll be glad to give Jack a ride home." *I couldn't have said that better myself.*

After everyone had left, the waiters and waitresses got busy cleaning up around us, so we got the hint and left. On leaving Taco Taco, Diana asked, "So where do you live?"

When I told her, she grinned and said, "I should be able to find that. My apartment is in the very next development." We grinned at the realization that we were practically next-door neighbors. When we were in front of my apartment, an awkward silence developed with my having the problem of getting out the next question. Diana was the one who broke the silence. "Shall I pick you up for church next week?"

"That will be great! I'll be looking forward to that." Then I remembered that when I became a full programmer, per corporate policy business cards were made for me with my name, title and home and office number printed on them. I got one out of my wallet and gave it to her. Taking the card from me, she very prettily asked, "Thank you. Do you have a second one?"

Reaching back into my wallet, I replied, "Yes, sure." I handed her another card. She dug into her purse, found a pen and wrote her name and number on the back of the second card and gave it back, "So call me."

I did, and the following Friday we went on our first date; to the movies, where we saw *Summer Rental,* a comedy with John Candy.

On one of our dates, we went to Six Flags amusement park, which back then was very new and not as fancy as today. In fact, just two years before it first opened, it had been a failing wild animal drive-through preserve.

While there, I saw this very tall water slide that looked like a lot of fun. "Diana, let's check this out."

"But the line looks so long," Diana commented.

"The line appears to be moving quickly. Let's get in line. It looks like a lot of fun." So we did.

About halfway up this very long, very high stairway to the top, I heard a guy behind me say, "This line is so long. It's taking too long to get to the top."

The guy right behind me answered, "Don't worry. It's about this time the cowardly chicken shits start losing their nerve and start walking back down the stairs, making the line shorter and the wait shorter as well."

As if on cue, Diana, who was in the stairway line ahead of me and had not heard them, turned to me and announced, "I'm sorry, Jack, but this is just getting too high for me. I'm going to walk back down."

"Would you like me to go back down the stairs with you?" I asked, being the gentleman.

"No, you go on up, and I will be waiting for you at the bottom."

Just then I heard the guy behind me say, "See, a real chicken-shit heading down the stairs."

I turned to the guy and, emphasizing each word, said, "That real chicken shit is my date. You will apologize very quickly and very sincerely." Glancing over the stairway railing, about ten to twenty feet down, I added, "Or you may arrive down the stairs a lot faster than my lady will."

He got the message and really did sound as if his apology was sincere. When Diana started walking back down the stairs, I gave her lots of room and so did the guys. In fact everyone was giving Diana a lot of room as she walked back down, just as if she were Princess Diana, after all she was my princess. How did I know about everyone moving out of her way, all the way down the stairs? In her red one-piece bathing suit she was quite the hot view, all the way down the stairs.

I enjoyed the slide down and at the bottom, before I even got out of the water, I was lovingly attacked by my Princess Diana.

Six months later we spent Christmas with her mother and sister in Ohio. Our plans were to get there by train. I ordered tickets for the both of us. I made a point of giving the ticket person on the phone both of our single names for the tickets. I even made the lady repeat it back. So of course, the tickets came for "Mr. & Mrs. Jack Poisner." On the train I joked, "Well, as the train has pronounced us 'man and wife' shall we consummate our marriage?" [Planes have their "One Mile Club" for those who have sex on planes; what do trains have?]

Diana just smiled at the joke, a proper lady like response to such a suggestive joke.

Diana grew up in one of those small towns where everyone knew everyone, so she introduced me to lots of friends. At one point, we were crossing the street within a crosswalk when something strange happened. There was nothing around us; the closest homes were a block away and there was nothing but fields around us. As we crossed the street I heard a car slow to a stop at least a half a block away. *Strange.*

Pointing the car out to Diana, I asked, "What is he doing?"

"Being courteous," she answered.

To my genuine surprise I answered, "Man, I am not used to that."

It was a lovely visit. Her mother could not have been more charming and great to be around. I felt strange sleeping nights in her bed, but she swore she spent more nights sleeping on the couch than she did in her own bed anyway. Diana slept in her old bed in a room she grew up sharing with her sister, Chris.

Two months later, I gave her a computer printout that was a poem that asked her to marry me and have my children. Computer printouts outside a computer complex were rare. I thought she would be impressed with the uncommonness of it. Eagerly waiting for an answer she simply said, "It does not rhyme well."

About a month later, on my birthday she gave me a birthday card that had inked in very large print, "YES" inside.

Six months later we were married. One of my fondest memories of our wedding day, I did not even learn about until years later. We had agreed not to shove wedding cake into each other's face, so when I went to feed Diana her piece of cake I took careful aim for her mouth. I succeeded in this performance *only because as the cake was about to go up her nose, she quickly went up on her toes so the cake made it to her mouth.*

After we married, she moved into my apartment. Eventually, with two incomes, we started looking for a house we could afford. When we started to look around, Diana said, "Jack, you know the bad shape my mother's house is in—it's falling apart around her. Then she has to take care of my sister, Chris, with her birth-related disability. Mom's only job is a part-time job that's a four hour round-trip. Lately, she's been having some health problems of her own. Do you think we could find a house big enough that my mother and sister could move in with us?" I assumed as Diana was the oldest of six, she felt the most responsible for her mother and sister.

The health problem was news to me. She seemed healthy during our visit. With concern, I asked, "What is this health problem? I don't recall her having any problem, other than her bad back, when we were visiting with her during Christmas."

"It started shortly after Christmas. I don't know all the details as she is reluctant to talk about it. What do you think, about my mother and sister moving in with us?"

After giving it some thought and seeing no problems, I said, "I think your mother is something special, like her daughter. Your sister and I sure hit it off when I visited for Christmas. If we can find a place big enough and affordable, I see no problem in having them move in with us."

We did find a place big enough. Our future home had two bedrooms on the ground floor, one bigger than the other. When we viewed the house, the bigger room was being used as an office. I could easily see using the room as a bedroom, as this "office" came with its own closet. With two more large bedrooms upstairs, that gave us enough bedrooms for mother-in-law and sister-in-law on the ground floor, and upstairs, one for Diana and me and one room for a child. We figured if we had two children, one boy and one girl, the girl could share a room with her live-in Auntie.

Her mother, Elaine, and sister, Chris, were indeed no problem at all. All newlyweds have their adjustment period. While we never fought, we did have our arguments, some more heated than others. It always impressed me that Diana's mother refused to get in the middle of our marital conflicts. I did quickly learn that I had to watch my tone anywhere near Chris; if I raised my voice she would run off and bury herself in her room—something to do with her upbringing with her father. You'll never hear any mother-in-law jokes from me. Unfortunately it turned out my mother-in-law was even sicker than any of us knew, and a little over a year after she moved in with us, we were back in Ohio giving this fine lady her final rest.

Over the years, my workplace had developed, and my boss enjoyed showing off this work area. Going from left to right, there was a copier with all its controls that were wired to a Kurzweil reader with its control panel. (Papers and paperbacks fed to the copier would be verbally read by the Kurzweil, while a copy would be saved within the computer.) The Kurzweil was wired to my PC, so that what was read to me from the copier went to the IBM PC. The PC had its keyboard, plus a Jaws control panel so I could tell the PC how I wanted information on the PC screen voiced [output] to me. Next to the PC was a CCTV magnifier with its dials and switches that could vastly magnify specs for programs under development. Next to the CCTV was a printer with all its controls. My boss just loved showing off *my cockpit*. Eventually, someone went so far as to add a poster of an airline cockpit to the wall behind my equipment.

Everyone in our department was an internal programmer, designing programs and program systems for other departments within the corporation. Most programs eventually were exported onto computers within these other departments for their use. Some programs were developed for other departments that we kept and used to run report updates for them either quarterly or yearly. Some of these programs continued to use mainframe tapes as a source of data input; some required our manual input through the keyboard. The CCTV magnifier was very useful on these jobs.

While my peripheral vision continued to decay, my central vision remained the same. Since the major loss of vision, my central vision had developed a new problem. Use of my vision for reading would tire my eyesight quickly. I have always been a bookworm, but now I was using the Kurzweil for both program development and leisure reading. As I am an ardent reader of horror books, I'd get comments from my fellow programmers who would complain how I was grossing them out.

To keep my bookworm fed, I also became a member of *Talking Book Topics.*

Talking Book Topics is a Library of Congress program to supply reading material for the blind and physically handicapped in the form of Braille books, books on records and books on cassettes. Special equipment is needed and provided for the records and books on cassettes. The records play at a special slow speed; while the books on cassettes play at a special slow speed and on four tracks (instead of the normal two tracks). All these materials come as "Material for the Blind and Physically Handicapped" and are delivered and returned in the mail at no cost. (Later, in the new millennium, books on records are long gone history. Cassette books are being phased out for the new digital book system. With the new digital system, you can still get books mailed to you to be used with your digital book reader, or you may download books onto your computer and move them to your digital book machine using a flash card.)

In the mid-90's my wife and I were gifted with a beautiful two-headed daughter. Being female, she was quite stubborn about coming out of her nice warm mother, so much so that the doctor had to use tongs to help pull her out. With my poor eyesight, the use of the tongs gave her a two-headed look that they promised me would be gone by the next day. True to their word, the next day my beautiful little girl had only one head; I know because I checked. It did not escape me that I still had the eyesight to enjoy seeing my daughter's birth.

Two months before our family was to grow by one, I was laid off. The corporation had been fighting for its existence for years and, losing the fight, had sold itself to another corporation; a corporation that already had its own department of internal programmers, so it axed my whole department right up to the VP. We were just the first to go. Today the corporation that had been so good to me for seventeen years no longer exists.

With my wife having the higher salary as an executive secretary, and as I was wrestling with my sleep apnea, it was decided that I would go on disability, be a Mr. Mom, and take care of our daughter with the assistance of my sister-in-law, Chris. Seems she was a babysitter back in Ohio, mainly because she lived in such a small town that no matter where she was babysitting, if there was an emergency she could always go next door for help. So here she could help with her niece, even if I was busy in bed trying to get some quality sleep. If an emergency would come about she only had to wake me. Wouldn't you know the only emergency we had with Elaine came while I was the only one home with her. Chris had fed her, but had to leave before Elaine had received her juice. I was asked to give Elaine her juice, and then let her out of her high chair. While drinking her juice, Elaine started choking and wheezing. I got her out of her high chair and started pounding her back at an angle that I hoped would free whatever she was chocking on, but not hurt her. (I knew it was dangerous to give a baby or young child the Heimlich maneuver.) I rushed her to the couch and, after sitting her down, I ran back into the kitchen and grabbed up the phone to call 911.

After I got off the phone, I noticed my little darling was just sitting there with her arm in her mouth, looking as if she was wondering if Daddy had just gone nuts. She was never a thumb sucker; instead she would put her arm in her mouth and suck on it.

EMS arrived and found that all was well. Just the same, they suggested she be seen by her doctor, so that evening we saw the baby doctor. During the visit, we figured out what had happened. Chris had given her raisins with her lunch. One of the raisins had gotten lodged in her gums and had come loose when she was drinking her juice.

Just a note on white cane use I believe is required due to moviemakers that don't bother researching things like the lifestyle of the blind. Blind people do not use a white cane getting around their own home. We might not even use the white cane in other places outside our home which are well known to us. For example, I don't use my white cane while visiting my parents. This can sometimes be painful, for instance when someone leaves a dining-room chair out or makes a change in the living room furniture and forgets to tell the blind member of the family of the changes. At work, I was introduced to a fellow blind employee who was now totally blind from RP. He told me that he had gotten into the habit of leaving his white cane behind when going to the men's room. He would walk out of the office, feel the hallway wall, then feel his way to the rest rooms. He always knew what door to use, because in his building, all the men's room doors opened to the left and all the women's rooms opened to the right. One day while feeling his way down the hallway, he painfully discovered, nose first, that someone in the next department was getting a new desk and that the old desk was sitting propped up at an angle against the hallway wall. His hand had slipped between the wall and the desk. He also told me that after his department had moved to a new building, the left-right rest room door system failed him as he walked into a left opening door and a bunch of female employees yelled, "Eric, you're in the wrong rest room." Eric just responded, "No problem, I can't see anything." He was quickly escorted out.

I had a similar experience once. While vacationing in Florida and visiting Epcot Center, I overheard a man say he was going to use the men's room. It sounded like a good idea, so I told my wife I was going to use the men's room. "Need help finding it?" she asked.

"No, I'm just going to follow that man in."

It was a bright, sunny day and the man was wearing dark clothes. I figured I could handle it. When I followed the person into the rest room, a crowd of women all started screaming—somehow I followed the wrong person right into the ladies' room. I did not know women could scream in so many accents.

With the purchase of the house, our finances had become tight. The plain was for both Diana and I to grow in our careers with this growth including higher wages and more income. It had not been in our plains for me to go on disability.

With me on disability, money was getting even tighter, too tight(er). We spend nights tossing around varies ideas to bring in more money. Nothing seemed plausible, things were looking down right depressing until …

We started talking about renting out the room that had previously been used by my mother-in-law. It was now basically an unused guest room. As we don't have that many over-night guests, an extremely unused guest room.

My wife had some reservations.

The first problem was that with a household of mostly women there were concerns about renting a room to a strange man. The solution was that the renter would have to be a female.

Another problem was that a renter would want some use of the refrigerator. Our refrigerator was already overused, was often full and was showing its age (yet another reason to look for additional income). The solution was to buy a bigger refrigerator. So once we decided that a renter was a plausible solution, we took money from savings and with financing, we bought a bigger refrigerator that even had the capacity to be sectioned so the renter could have her own area within the refrigerator.

Diana placed ads in the paper and interviewed possible candidates for the room. I lost track of how many came and went because Diana saw some problem with them.

With potential renters coming and going faster than I change my socks, I was beginning to believe there never would be a renter. It was beginning to look like no one could live up to my wife's standards as a renter.

I had become so busy with the local Chapter of NFB (National Federation of the Blind) that I was voted in as VP. My first duty was to help organize bake sales during the Memorial Day weekend to help raise money to get members to the yearly NFB convention, to be held in Dallas, Texas, this year. It was my job to go to various shops and ask permission to set up our bake sales. As we have been doing this for years, in the same locations without any problems, this was a piece of cake.

I'd only been to two conventions in the past. One was in D.C. so being basically local, I had no need for a hotel room, and no food cost to worry about. The second convention I attended was in Florida. Since it was the summer after I got married, Diana and I, while attending some of the meetings that most interested me, mostly made a vacation of it. This year I felt strongly about going as my duty in my role as VP. Fortunately as VP, the chapter would be covering some of my costs. This year the bake sales went so well that most of my costs were subsidized. About a dozen members who wanted to attend this year's convention did attend, including six who would not have been able to afford to go without the help of people who not only bought up our home-baked cakes, pies and cookies, but left generous donations as well.

With the convention two months away, life went on, with my wife going to work; me trying to get some decent sleep due to the sleep apnea, and Chris and I taking care of little Elaine. Chris was great with baby Elaine, except she refused to change dirty diapers. That duty fell on daddy or mommy when they were home. One day, I walked into the living room to find Auntie Chris sitting down to a movie while baby Elaine enjoyed her toys in her playpen. When the credits for *Nightmare on Elm Street* came up, I looked at baby Elaine and quickly decided this was not a good idea. Auntie Chris agreed and found something a little more family-oriented to watch. About a year or so later, I brought home a used copy of Chuck Norris (Saturday type) cartoons called Chuck Norris: Karate Kommandos. Elaine and I watched them together, until during the 3rd cartoon, I discovered that my little girl was kickboxing her teddy bear. I watched the rest of the cartoons on the VHS after my little kickboxer was down for a nap.

The possible renters interviewed by Diana for the guest room just kept coming and going. I got to figuring we were in no danger of losing a guest room anytime soon.

One weekday morning I awoke to the sounds of my wife getting ready for work. I was surprised to see it was so grey in the room, I recalled the weather man calling for a bright and sunny day. Possibly the weather man was wrong again. Instead of the sunny day called for, it looked like a dark, cloudy day, possibly with rain on the way, but I currently was hearing no pitter-patter of rain on the roof.

I said to Diana, "Di is the sun up yet?"

"It's just starting to get light out; that's why I have the bedside light on."

Looking in the direction of the bedside light and still seeing nothing but grayness, "Di?"

Hearing the concern creeping into my voice, I heard her stop what she was doing and answer, "Yes, Hon. What is it?"

"Di, I'm blind."

Thinking it some joke, she replied, "Yes, Hon, I know. I'm the one who takes you to John Hopkins for testing, remember."

"No Di." I continued, fighting to keep my voice from wobbling with the building emotion I was feeling, "I'm totally blind."

Chapter Four
Adjusting

I heard Diana rush around to the bedroom doorway, I heard her flick a switch, then rush to my side, announcing, "I just turned on the bedroom lights, can you see better now?" I could hear the concern in her voice as I felt the bed change as she sat down next to me. Her voice vibrated with so much concern I was tempted to lie and say, "Yes, that's better." or perhaps, "Oh, OK. My eyesight was just slow to wake up."

Sadly, I went with the truth, "No. all I see is grayness. Di, I'm totally blind. My eyesight is gone."

"Now wait, you have had periods of fatigue that weakened your eyesight so you couldn't see. Could this be what is happening?"

"I wish. No. During those times I still had light perception. Now I am not seeing anything but grayness—nothing." Flashing back to a similar visual experience, I added, "Di, remember when Johns Hopkins gave me color tests and the light grey was coming up more frequently?"

"Yes, a little."

"When the color gray started coming up more often during the color test, I asked why and was told, 'When you are seeing gray, what you are not seeing is the true color that is there. You are losing color perspective in the lighter color range. This is very common in people with RP.' Well Di, that grey is all I am seeing now. "

"I'll take the day off. We'll call your eye doctor and see what we can do. I'll run you up to John Hopkins, if that's what it takes." A frantic need to help was clogging her thoughts, as noted by the comment on driving me to John Hopkins. She hated city driving, any city, including Baltimore.

The Blind Vampire Hunter

As I reached out for Di's hand, her hands found mine, "Di... there is nothing the eye doctor can do. I have had yet another spurt of vision loss and now, as the doctors have warned us, I am totally blind. The RP has finally taken away what eyesight I had. I may never see again."

Real men don't cry. I refused to cry. Diana cried enough for the two of us.

Then baby Elaine cried. Diana said, "I guess I'd better go see to our little one." As I listened to Diana talking to Elaine and changing her diaper from the sound of it, I sat listening and thinking, *I guess I will never see those two again.* Over the years of research, so little seemed to be learned about RP that I really did not have much hope for a treatment, let alone a cure for RP. No, I figured my eyesight was gone and gone for good. It was time to adjust and go on.

Providentially, I had many years being legally blind, with one foot in the world of the sighted and one foot in the world of the blind. I sat hoping my slow vision loss was going to help me adjust to my total loss of vision. I figured this would make adjusting to total blindness easier as well. *Why me Lord, why me?*

One thing did surprise me...seeing grayness. I had always assumed that once I was totally blind, I'd see nothing but blackness.

I got up, put on some shorts and sandals I had laid out on and under my valet chair, then went down to put on the news. This was somewhat normal. Over the years of sitting around fatigued, I had become something of a news hound. I may have gotten this from my mother who, it was reported, woke up with the news, had lunch with the news (during her working at home years) and later went to bed with the news. I had not bothered to look at the TV remote to use it. I had not looked at the TV remote in years. While I couldn't tell you what all the labeled buttons are named, I could tell you what the buttons do by feeling the location, so turning on the TV was no trick.

I can't say I was really listening to the news that morning. I did not bother with breakfast; for some reason I just was not hungry. Even when Diana was finished with Elaine and asked what I'd like for breakfast, I answered, "Not hungry, thanks." I just went back to not seeing the news and, being mentally distracted, not listening to the news much.

Later, when Diana offered to fix me some lunch, I almost said, "OK." But instead I got the idea of fixing my own lunch. With Diana home, if I ran into problems I could call on her for help. So instead I answered, "I'll do it."

After I walked into the kitchen, I found the rack of plastic trays with little problem and moved to the counter. I carefully checked the counter with my free hand and discovered that it was cleaned off, so I put the tray down. So far, so good. I only had to feel a little in front of me to find the bread container and get out a couple of pieces of bread, again no problem.

Now I had to turn and walk two steps to the refrigerator and open it. Quickly finding the meat drawer, I opened it carefully, so I would not open it too far. Feeling around, I found the rounded package of bologna. I recalled that we sometimes got turkey or chicken slices in the same type of packaging. We'd have to work on that. The mustard was on the refrigerator door where it belonged, so I was set.

The trickiest part of fixing my lunch, while being totally blind, was getting the mustard on the meat and only on the meat. I believe I succeeded.

Leaving the kitchen, tray in hand, and heading for the stairway down to the family room, I bumped into one of the dining room chairs, not properly pushed in and kept on going. I recalled my boss who would call me *the human pinball* because of the way I'd bump into things and keep on going. As I headed down the stairs I heard the chair being pushed in. *Had Diana been watching me the whole time? How loving of her.*

Back downstairs in the family room, or as the family calls it "The Dungeon" because of all my horror décor, I had no problem finding my mini refrigerator and getting a canned drink from it. With my lunch gathered, I went to sit down to "watch" some news when I tripped slightly over one of baby Elaine's baby toys that Diana had left out from the night before.

Luckily, I kept my balance and made it to my lounge chair without further mishap. Once planted in my lounge chair, I started to eat my lunch and actually started listening to the news, as I was feeling a little better on the successful adventure in fixing my lunch within my new world of grayness.

The Blind Vampire Hunter

As I figured, adjusting to total blindness within the house was made easy from the many years of living with declining eyesight. Outside the house was a bit more difficult. It would take time to gain the experience and confidence in mobility as I had when legally blind.

I had a scheduled appointment with a dermatologist in two weeks. I had to think twice about keeping the appointment. Because of the potential importance of the appointment it was a no brainer. I would have to keep the appointment. I'm sure Diana would make a point about my keeping the appointment. Di had been bothering me for years about this mole on my back. If she had not mentioned it, I would not have even known it was there. When it got big enough that I could feel that it was there, I realized that meant it had to be growing. I called my doctor who gave me a referral for the dermatologist.

I first saw this doctor a week ago. She removed the growth and told me it would be sent to the lab for testing. At that time I got to the doctor's office using public transportation. Would I brave public transit totally blind as I did legally blind? If the appointment was today I would not, but in two weeks? We'll just have to wait and see.

Two weeks later, I kept the follow-up appointment thanks to help from Di. Today, I didn't use public transit on my own, not because of my fairly new total lack of sight, but because of fatigue, I was having a bad day due to the sleep apnea.

After the nurse led me into an exam room, allowing me to put my hand on her shoulder, I waited for the doctor, and waited, and waited. I was starting to get impatient enough to just leave, but after all, the dermatologist had used the "C" word (cancer) during my visit to have the mole removed. She said she thought it might be melanoma, a form of skin cancer that can be fatal if not caught early. I did not mention that the "mole" she removed had probably been part of my back for years. So, yes, I was nervous.

A slight knock on the closed exam door preceded the entrance of the dermatologist and interrupted my musings of my first visit. She entered with, "So, Mr. Poisner, what's new?"

"Well I'm blind," I answered.

As I heard her sitting down, she continued, "Yes, I remember you mentioning that you are legally blind."

"No, I mean I am now totally blind."

There was silence, then, "You did have some eyesight when I last saw you, right?" I heard concern and confusion in her voice.

Calmly, to keep things on the light side, I answered, "Yes. Since the last time I saw you I had a change in my eyesight that has left me totally blind."

"Have you informed your GP? Would you like me to inform your GP so a reference for consultation can be made with Mental Health?"

"No. I'm fine, adjusting still, but fine." Deliberately changing the subject to what was really concerning me right now, I asked, "So what can you tell me about that mole you removed?

With a pause, possibly to look at my file, she answered, "What was removed tested as malignant melanoma. While it was sizable, we did totally remove it. I believe you will not require any additional tests or procedures. Feel free to set up an appointment if any additional moles should develop, but I really doubt that will be necessary as I am sure we got all of this one. That's not to say that you can't develop a totally new one in the future." She walked over to me and took my hand to shake it, "Sure you don't need a referral to Mental Health?"

"I'm fine, especially after the good news that we are finished with that cancerous mole. Mind leading me out to the waiting area? My wife is there waiting for me." She did as I asked.

The morning came to fly to Dallas for the convention. While rechecking that I had packed everything I wanted to pack, Diana surprised me with, "By the way, I will be interviewing a young lady who just got a job down in D.C. Over the phone she sounded like a promising boarder."

I've heard that song before. I just said, "Aren't you driving me and the Russells to the airport?" "The Russells were the local NFB Chapter President and his wife, both born without eyes. During our last meeting, while in casual conversation it was discovered that the Pres., his wife, and I were taking the same flight to Dallas. On hearing this, Diana had volunteered to take them to the airport while with us, hence, saving our friends some cab fare.

"Yes of course, the interview isn't until tonight. I'll be back well before she arrives for our interview."

"What do you know about her?" I don't know why I asked. I'll probably never see her, as she'll most likely have some fault that will not get her past the interview. ("Never <u>see</u> her." We'd gotten into the habit of having one NFB meeting/picnic in the backyard each year. Di and her mother couldn't get over having twenty to thirty totally blind folk using phrases such as "I saw so and so last week," and "It's good to see you." For instance someone said, "Did you see how excited Paul got when he found out that he was going to Dallas for the convention?)

"She's starting a job down in D.C. managing a theatre. She's looking for something a bit more affordable than she can find down *in* D.C. She noted my ad mentioned *in walking distance of Metro, with easy access to D.C.*"

Interesting, we would have something in common. I had been a floor manager of a theatre during a year of college. Mostly I took tickets and oversaw the ushers. Sometimes I would do the walk. The walk consisted of walking the aisles and checking customers during the shows for bottles and smoking. With my night blindness, I discovered a system that worked for me; I would walk down to the front of the theatre and wait for a well-lit scene. Then I would walk back up the aisle, looking for the glint of the movie off bottle glass or the little flare of a smoking cigarette. My nose helped find smokers more often than my eyesight did. But then I waste my time; I'll never even see this woman boarder, she'll come and go like so many before her.

Later, we made it to the airport where airport staff was waiting for us with wheelchairs. "I'm sorry it's policy."

"A wheelchair for a blind person is *policy*?" I asked incredulously.

"Well, yes." he answered sounding slightly embarrassed.

"Does policy say we have to use these wheelchairs?" President Russell asked.

"Well, I guess not. I would be more comfortable if you individuals would use the wheelchairs, as it is policy."

"Tell me sir, would you feel right being wheeled around this airport in a wheelchair?" President Russell piped in.

"I guess not."

"And neither would we. We are handicapped, not disabled." President Russell declared,

The airport lackey finally got the point and ordered his two assistants to park the wheelchairs out of the way. He then asked, "Is it alright if we take your arms to help you?"

"That would be nice," President Russell answered.

I turned to Diana. "Well, I guess this is goodbye until I get back next week." I was going to miss my little Dolly Parton and her mini Dolly Parton, Elaine.

"It's just a week, and I will be right here waiting for you when you get back from your fun-filled week of conventioning."

One of the airport lackey's assistants then took my arm and we were off.

Word must have travelled faster than we did, as we were met at the Dallas airport by airport assistance, but they did not have wheelchairs for us blind. By the way, you'll be surprised how many sighted people speak loudly, even yell to the visually impaired, as if we are as deaf as we are blind.

Chapter Five
The Boarder

At the baggage pickup, the airport assistance was very pleasant, polite, and happy to hand over the blind to sighted volunteers provided by the Dallas Chapter of the NFB.

We arrived at the hotel that would also be the site for all the meetings I would be attending. I was checked in and given a name tag with my name in large print and Braille. I was shown to my room, which I would be sharing with Tom, another member of our local Chapter. The hotel employee volunteered to help put my things away, but I figured it would be wiser to do that myself, so I would know right where everything was. Tom must have felt the same way, as he also declined the special assistance.

With our belongings put in place, it was time to check out the facilities of the hotel. This meant testing the ridged map given out to all convention attendees, and I easily found one of the hotel restaurants and the room with the indoor pool. While exploring the indoor pool room, I discovered an unscheduled "I hate Dr. Funkenstein" meeting in progress. Dr. Funkenstein was the head researcher who had told my mother that I was going blind and it was all her fault. Some participants sitting poolside were mispronouncing his name as Dr. Frankenstein.

Later that night I called home and told Diana all about my day; after I had finished she had news for me. "We now have a boarder," she exclaimed excitedly.

"Oh, so tell me about her." I said with interest.

"Well, as I told you before you left, she was living in D.C. where the rent was killing her. She is just starting a new job managing a theatre.

She manages the theatre graveyard shift; that's to say, she manages the theatre during their special nightly showing of Japanese martial arts imports. These movies all start showings around midnight and go until early morning, depending on whether they are showing a double feature or a triple feature."

"Interesting. Maybe we should go down one night and pop in on her at work," I said.

"NO. I mean, we can't. It's in the agreement with her that we will at no time visit her place of employment."

"Strange."

"Not really, she works in a dangerous part of D.C. at a really dangerous time of night," Diana answered.

"Wait, *she* works in a dangerous part of D.C. during a most dangerous time of the night?" I responded incredulously.

"Yes, but it's OK, for her; she is a Master of Kung Fu. She has been studying it most of her life. In fact, before she could get the job, she had to be tested in her Kung Fu proficiency and prove her ability to defend herself and others. Seems some audience members get carried away by the martial art movies and start fights within the theatre. It's a qualification that all employees of the graveyard shift be well trained in martial arts, as they may have to double as bouncers during the movies. She's been told it's quite common. During her first month as manager, she has had to stop a fight once or twice a week. She said she has been in some in-theatre fights that have already tested her talents in her Kung Fu training… No, we will not be going down to see her at anytime," Diana proclaimed emphatically.

Remembering one of her big concerns, I asked, "So how goes the sharing of the refrigerator?"

"We don't. She has a mini frig in her room, much like the one you have in the family room downstairs, and she eats most of her meals out. She has gotten into the practice of getting breakfast at an IHOP near where she works while waiting for the subway to start up in the morning to get her back here. She told me that after the theatre is closed for the graveyard showings, she uses the quiet time to keep up with the paperwork, and then she gets breakfast at IHOP. Sometimes she does paperwork while she is eating her breakfast."

"Interesting. So what do you think of...what is her name? You have never given me her name."

"Her name is Isabella Báthory. Isn't that just such a charming name?" Diana answered with a sound of envy sneaking into her voice. "It's just so...old English."

Somehow that name sounds familiar. Isabella Bathory Isabella Bathory, old English. Perhaps it's a name from history? Right, you have someone famous person wanting to move into your guest room so they can afford to manage a theater at night. Yah, that really works.

So why does that name sound so familiar?

Breaking into his deliberations, "She is just so lovely, you should see her. She's a tall, lean blond with such perfect light skin tone. I swear I just don't know why she is not making a career as an actress or at least as a model. She has such a lovely angelic voice. I have already tried to talk her into joining the church choir, but she reminded me that she works Saturday nights into Sunday morning so while church is in session, she is getting some well needed sleep."

Interesting. I have known her to repeatedly turn down potential boarders because they were not churchgoers. It also came to me that as a young twenty-something, I had a friend who worked guard duty so late into Sunday morning that he would arrive at church still in his uniform. He just barely had time to rush directly to church. He come in uniform because he did not have even enough time to change before the Sunday services began, but at least he came to church.

So our new boarder is not a church attendee, but she is still renting a room in our home. How interesting. Now that I think of it, I don't recall Di ever talking about a woman's looks the way she talks about this Isabella Báthory. She must be quite a woman.

The next night after a full day of meetings, I was so tired I just couldn't call home. The phone call would have to wait until tomorrow night. My inability to call home was disturbing considering I missed one meeting while getting a nap for the sole purpose of making it through the rest of the day awake and mentally alert. In my last working years before my whole department get laid off, I usually got some sleep during lunch to get me through the rest of the day without having to battle the fatigue brought on by the sleep apnea.

The following night I made a point of calling home. (I was also feeling a little guilty for not calling the night before.) Besides I was missing my beautiful wife and daughter.

When I got her on the phone and after we shared our separate activities of the day with each other, I remembered a concern I had about the boarder, "Di, I'm thinking with our boarder working nights and sleeping days, am I going to have to pussy foot around my own home during the day so as not to disturb her daytime sleeping?"

Di laughed, "When I came home today; I could hear music blasting inside the house before I could even get to the front door. I burst into the house to find Chris with the stereo blaring. My first thought was, "Isabella is going to absolutely have a fit.""

"Oh no, did she?" I asked fearing what was coming.

"Not a bit. When I apologized for the loud music, she responded,"What loud music?""

"When I told her of what I found when I came home from work she simply waved a hand of dismissal and said, 'don't worry about being quiet during the day. I sleep like the dead.'"

"That was nice and polite of her," I interjected.

"No, Hon, I believe her. I really think that she can sleep so soundly that she could sleep through just about anything. So don't worry about having to be especially quiet during the day because of Isabella's sleeping."

"So Issy is a very sound sleeper." I mused, a little relieved, if this was true.

"NO."

I was startled by the sound of sudden panic that came through the phone. Di continued, "Don't you ever call her Issy, EVER. Her name is Isabella or Isabella Báthory. Never Isse or Issy or anything else. DO YOU UNDERSTAND ME?"

"OK, I get the message." *But not the overreaction.*

"You had better, mister."

She was really serious about the pronouncing of Iss—I mean Isabella's name. I'd better remember or Di sounds like she will take my head off.

Changing back to her loving tone that I love so well, she continued, "It's late and I have meetings all day tomorrow. Let's call it a night so the both of us can get some sleep. Speaking of sleep, how are you getting by with your sleep apnea and all those meetings?"

"Well, I nap during lunch break, and I did fall asleep during one of the meetings, but overall, I'm not doing badly. When I mentioned to Tom that I fell asleep during the afternoon meetings, he said I wasn't alone by far. We both got a laugh at that."

"Well, I'll say goodnight and sleep tight." With that she gave me a kiss over the phone. The phone clicked, and the connection went dead.

Wednesday was a "meeting free" day, a day for taking tours or just taking a break from the meetings. Tom was part of a large group that went to Six Flags. On their return, a number of the Six Flag goers were reported as not feeling well from dehydration. My roommate, Tom, was one of them.

But for me, I had special plans. Before leaving home I had noted that my Baltimore Orioles were in town to play the Texas Rangers, so I came prepared. I took a taxi to the Rangers' stadium all ornamented with my Orioles' cap, shirt and leather belt and shiny matching belt buckle. I was ready to watch my Baltimore boys trump the Rangers. I had everything but a ticket. With the Rangers having a losing season, and the O's on a winning streak, I figured I would not have any trouble getting a ticket because of lackadaisical attendance that losing brings on among some fans...

Boy, I could not have been more right. Getting out of the taxi all duded up in my O's gear, a man on the sidewalk asked me in a Texas twang, "You's here for the game?"

Not being able to hide my excitement, I replied, "Sure am."

"Put your hand out, son." So I did.

He put a slip of paper the right size and shape to be a game ticket in my outstretched hand, and said, "That's a little old ticket for the game. Have a good time on me."

I sure did, especially as my boys of Baltimore beat the Rangers with a score I'd be too embarrassed for the sake of my Texas friends to mention. I also got back to the hotel not suffering from dehydration. I was not suffering at all.

Friday night was Banquet Night and while it was fun, it just was not the same as the one in Florida with my Di. That night, Diana and I had stepped onto the dance floor together for the first time. We had figured, with most of the dancers being blind, who would notice a couple of novices faking it on the dance floor.

Saturday morning was scheduled for packing luggage for those who had flights that same day. My flight back, with the Russells was scheduled for late afternoon. While the same treatment of airport assistance was given, no wheelchairs were offered to us.

At BWI (Baltimore Washington International) they also did not arrive to assist us with wheelchairs, instead they had a multi-seat golf cart customized for airport use to put us all in. We were all so tired from a busy week, which finished off with partying until morning, that the customized golf cart treatment seemed a real delight.

After riding over to pick up our luggage, we were driven out into the pickup area. Nothing else sounds like the pickup area of an airport. There was the traffic noise and the sounds of hassled people getting picked up or dropped off while trying to keep track of their luggage. There were also the public announcements. They were not as humorous as portrayed in the comedy *Airplane!*, Jer' did get a grin out of remembering how, in the movie, there were two public announcers, a man and a woman. The public announcements decayed into a continuation of an argument the two must have had while on a date. He continued his happy thoughts of the movie, remembering a another line, "And don't call me Shirley."

Diana must have waved down our airport version of a golf cart's driver, as he drove us right up to her car. While Diana helped us into the car, the airport assistant loaded up the trunk of the car with our luggage.

The first stop was to the Russells' home to drop them and their luggage off. We were a more subdued group in the car, leaving BWI, than we were driving to BWI a week earlier. Us party animals were just too partied out – well, until I got my wife home that is. After all it had been a whole week.

Chapter Six
Meeting Isabella Bathory, Boarder

You can believe we made up for the week of abstinence before the luggage was even unpacked.

While helping me unpack, Diana found the western style top I bought her. It was similar to the blouse the sales lady was wearing. She suggested I have a closer look to see for myself just how sexy a top it was, even to taking my hand and showing the low cleavage of the neckline. Later, when Diana put her gift on, she proved the sales lady was right, as attested by the sudden tightness in my pants. For baby Elaine, there was a cowboy bunny rabbit wearing a complete western outfit, including a wide brim hat with big bunny ears coming through the hat's brim.

After we finished unpacking, Diana put on her new western top and nothing else and the horizontal bed boogie began all over again. Man, that saleswoman was right. That was one sexy top. Hey, can you blame us for acting like two teens in the back of father's car. After all it had been a whole week.

Afterward, while lying in bed feeling as contented as a cowboy in a whore house, I asked, "So when do I meet our new boarder?"

Diana, also sounding as contented as a well paid whore in a Texas whore house, took a minute to answer. She looked at the bedside clock and answered, "I guess tomorrow morning, if you're up early enough. She's already gone to work by now."

The next morning I awoke to, "Hey, sleepy head, time to get up." When I reached out to grab her, she jumped back, laughing. "Now none of that. I let you sleep in as long as feasible. But now you have to get up and get dressed so we can get to church on time." The last part sounded like a song, especially coming from the sweet voice of my lovely wife.

"So do I get to meet Miss Isabella Báthory, Boarder?"

"Sorry, no." She sounded disturbed.

"Something wrong?" I asked, concerned about the tone in her voice.

"Not really. She has already come in from work, showered and got to bed for the day. She wanted to stay up and meet you, but she had a rough night of it and needed to get to bed."

"So why do you sound worried?"

"Not worried per se. I just get a little disturbed when she comes home with blood on her clothes."

"Blood! What the hell are you talking about?" I replied, almost raising my voice.

"Oh, it's happened before. Some movie goer gets carried away with the martial arts movie, sees himself as the unbeatable and starts a fight right there in the theatre. Then Isabella and her ushers have to play bouncer to the over-enthusiastic patron. In this case the guy pulled a knife and attacked Isabella. She had no choice but to take him down."

"And the blood?"

"His. It seems he fell on his blade during the fight. She told me the police had to be called, as well as an ambulance. It was one of those rough nights she sometimes has. It's not the first time she has come home with blood on her clothes. Oh, EMS told her the knife wielder will be alright after some rest, a transfusion, and then it's off to jail for that creep."

I don't think I have ever heard my sweet Di call anyone a "creep" before. Just didn't seem right somehow.

At church, many said how they missed me last Sunday, as I was in Texas at the convention. The convention did provide a unification service last Sunday morning, or you could just sleep in before the first meeting that Sunday afternoon. A unification service just seemed too strange to me so I decided to sleep in. For now, Reverend Bob gave a sermon on the Prodigal Son that got me wondering if he was preaching to me for not being present at church the week before. *Had anyone mentioned to him about the convention I was attending? Now I'm just being silly.*

The Blind Vampire Hunter

I was reminded of something that happened during my high school years. During a youth Saturday morning outing, I broke my arm, but good. The doctor made the mistake of using the "S" (surgery) word. After it took three nurses and two doctors to hold me and calm me down, the doctor decided he would only set and cast my arm, not surgically pin it. "Now, you go home and stay in bed for three days. You don't get out of bed for any reason, and move that arm as little as possible," the doctor ordered very seriously. Doing as he said, Sunday morning I was in bed listening to the Sunday service on the radio, when the preacher got up to give the sermon and announced, "I don't think I can do the sermon this morning. Young Jack Poisner, who is always sitting in the second row every Sunday, is not here with his ever-present smiling face, as he is home with a broken arm." Of course, he did give his sermon. When I got back to school, I was really surprised how many and, in some cases, who had heard my name on the radio. My mind almost screamed, *Jack, the sermon.* Right, enough, no more with the mind wandering as Reverend Bob went on with his sermonizing on the Prodigal Son.

That evening I got to finally meet our boarder for the first time. As Di and I were sitting in the living room playing with baby Elaine, I heard the creak of Isabella Báthory opening the front door. *One of these days we really have got to do something about that door.*

I listened to her coming into the room. *Did the room just get colder?* I heard Di announce, "Isabella, you're looking better than you did this morning."

"Yes, a good day's sleep does wonders for me," Isabella answered.

My mind screamed, *My god! Was that from the beautiful Isabella Báthory, with the voice of an angel, that I had been hearing about?* That voice. That incredible voice. That gravel-filled voice sounded as if it came right out of hell itself.

Chapter Seven
Best Bud, Eric

It was all I could do to keep from cringing at the sound of that voice from hell. I must have heard wrong. I must have. All the raving *from Di wishing to get Isabella into the church choir because of her angelic voice and she sounds like that. Something is not right.*

Getting up from my seat to properly meet the new element within the family, I said, "Hi, I'm Jack." Since I was about to meet a woman for the first time, I was not sure whether I should put my hand out or not, so I just casually put it between us, giving her the option of taking my hand or not taking my hand to be shaken in greeting.

The room did get colder as the voice from hell said, "Hi Jack, I'm Isabella Báthory." There was an uneasy silence. She broke it with a screech that almost destroyed my hearing with its pure ugliness, "YOU'RE BLIND."

I wanted to respond very violently with an ax to her head. It wasn't because of her "blind" comment, for it was a comment not a question, and I have heard it many times before. I suddenly had this feeling of sudden rage. It was like something I felt once when I was in college. It was the first day of classes, and I was taking public transportation to my college in D.C. Halfway there, the bus stopped to pick up this guy that was your stereotypical hippie from the headband, to the psychedelic vest over an undershirt, right down to his sandals. Seeing him, I had a sudden urge to get out of my seat and pummel this guy into a large, bloody pile. Like to freak me out. I have nothing against hippies or this stranger, so the whole thing took me by surprise. The next day we picked up this hippie, and again, I wanted to tear him to shreds. At least, this time I knew why. He was wearing the same outfit as the day before, except he was also wearing a black upside-down cross necklace—he was a Satan worshipper. My soul sensed it, but it was my body that reacted. The feeling I felt with this boarder was déjà vu to my senses.

I heard her rush out of the room. There was a definitive chill in the air as she rushed past me, leaving the screen door to slam shut behind her. The graveyard chill of many deaths in the air left with her. I stood there with my skin trying to crawl for cover, totally confused and bewildered.

I looked in the direction of Di and in my confusion asked, "What happened?"

She just answered, dreamily, "She must have had to rush off to work. What a shame. Is not her voice just so angelic? It's a shame I can't talk her into becoming a part of the church choir."

My incredulousness over what she had said and what had just happened must have shown on my face and was misconstrued by Diana as she added, "Yes, I know, she works Saturday nights and is not able to attend church. What a shame."

I remembered from my Bible studies that Satan was, and most likely is still, a very beautiful angel in appearance, presumably with a very angelic voice. I tended to agree that the voice I heard was from an angel alright—an angel kicked out of heaven—an angel from hell.

I heard Di go back to playing with Elaine, and I got to wondering how that horrid voice could sound so extremely beautiful to Di and sound so horribly painful to me. Could Di be so blind to what is living in our home? ... Or is she living? ... *Blind.* "Di, did you not mention to our boarder that I am blind?"

"Now that you mention it, I guess it just never came up," Diana answered. She continued, "I think of you as my loving husband, not as my blind husband. I guess it just never occurred to me to mention it to her."

She continued, "She must have been running late for the bus, to have rushed out the way she did. Usually we have a little time to talk before she runs off to work"

It also just occurred to me that the room got back to being warm again. Could the room temperature really have changed while this boarder was in the room or was that just my imagination? RIGHT. Like I imagined that painful voice, that voice that Di keeps harping about being so lovely.

Just then I heard the screen door open again. *Is she returning for some reason? It will be interesting to see if the room temperature changes again.* I made a point of feeling for a change in the room temperature as the approaching footsteps entered into the living room from outside. *The room temperature is not changing.*

"Hey, Jack, it's Eric, man. So how was your trip?

Getting up to put out a hand, I returned the greeting, "Eric, my man, how's it hanging?"

"Jack, watch what you say in front of the baby," Diana corrected.

"I can't. I'm blind." Old joke, but I couldn't pass it up.

Looking back in Eric's direction, I continued, "The trip was great, but tiring ..."

"You did not seem so tired in the bedroom after you got back," Diana quipped.

Faking shock, I answered jokingly, "Honey, watch what you are saying in from of the baby."

After we all laughed that one off, the conversation got back to my trip. When I mentioned the incident with the wheelchairs, Eric said, "Some things never change. When I got back from 'Nam with my shattered arm in a cast, I was greeted at the airport with a wheelchair. With all of my luggage and only the use of one arm, I took them up on it."

Changing the subject, I asked Eric, "So what do you think of our new boarder?"

"Man, you are one lucky stiff. No way would my wife trust me with a babe like that in the same house. No way man. Have you seen the knockers on her?"

"Eric!" Diana demanded,

"Yeah, I know, not in front of the baby," Eric answered.

"No, not in front of *me*." We laughed all over again.

"Di, you have nothing to be concerned about in that area," I put in while still laughing.

"So you have met her, our new boarder?" I asked Eric.

"Yep, you might have noticed, I was not allowed to come over to see my bud until after my wife saw her leave for work. Hey, did she seem to leave here in a hurry?"

"Jack thinks she might have been disturbed at finding out that he's blind," Diana put in.

"Well, maybe she had not had much experience around blind folk where she comes from. Maybe it took her totally by surprise. I take it, Diana, that you didn't think to mention it to her?"

"No, I did not," Dianna answered pointedly.

Getting back to my original question, I asked again, "So Eric, what do you think of her, besides her knockers, I mean?"

Diana interrupted, "Guys, if you keep up the talk about the knockers, I'M LEAVING."

"I think she's impressive. To have come all the way over here from Central Europe to make a life for herself, basically alone. That takes spunk. Strange though, you know my fascination with vampires and vampire lore, hell, all things vampire. Well, with her being from Romania, known as the old Transylvania territory of Dracula, I tried several times to talk to her about her home grounds and vampires, but she changed the subject on me … every time. She's made it very clear that this is not something she wants to talk about. I do think it even stranger, that when she mentioned her job at the theatre, I asked if she would get me in for free if I came down. She literally begged me not to come down to the theatre. She said it would be too dangerous. When I mentioned my two tours of duty in 'Nam she still insisted I never come down to her place of business. She again said the area is too dangerous."

"She made it a part of our agreement that we would never go down to her place of employment, because it could be too dangerous to do so. You do know she's a Master of Kung Fu and has even won tournaments with her fighting ability," Diana reminded us.

"You know what? In the news there has been a rash of murders down in her area lately. But when isn't someone getting iced down in D.C.?" I added.

Eventually Eric headed back to his wife and baby boy. He made an interesting comment once about my baby girl and his baby boy, "You know, when my little boy grows up, all I have to worry about is my one boy, but when your little girl grows up you will have to worry about *all the boys.*"

We put baby Elaine to bed and soon went to bed ourselves. I had trouble getting to sleep that night, and it was not because of my sleep apnea.

The next morning, by the time I had gotten up, our live-in Auntie, Chris, informed me that Isabella Báthory had already gotten home and was in bed for the day. It was just another day in the life of the Poisners. That evening when Diana came home, I asked her to call me upstairs from the family room when her dear Isabella woke so Isabella and I could get to know each other better.

Eventually Di called me up for dinner and as I sat down, I asked, "So when does Isabella get up? Isn't it about that time?"

"Oh, she's gone already," Diana calmly, matter-of-factually answered. "She's already off to work."

Trying to keep my cool, I asked, "So why didn't you call me so I could talk with Isabella?"

"She said she did not have the time and would have to rush to work." Then dinner was served, and nothing more was said about our boarder. Nothing more was said *out loud.* Inwardly I fumed over Diana's failure to do as I asked. I fumed over Isabella succeeding in avoiding me. All this fuming only added gas to a burning house.

Chapter Eight
The Fire

Whoop, whoop, whoop.

What the hell, ... the smoke detector.

Whoop, whoop, whoop.

Diana must be burning dinner again. Wait a minute. I hit the button on my watch. "The time is three-o-nine p.m.," the female voice of my watch announced. It's too early for Di to be fixing dinner. Shit, could the house be on fire?

Whoop, whoop, whoop.

Jumping out of my lounge chair and ignoring the news, I rushed carefully around the family room couch and made my way as fast, but as carefully as possible. Finding the stairway, I rushed up the stairs to find Diana coming out of the kitchen. Seeing me, she yelled, "There's a fire in the kitchen."

Whoop, whoop, whoop. The smoke detector was sounding in the hallway leading to the stairway down to the family room. I was standing practically right under the smoke detector, and it was even louder now.

Looking into the service square, a square cut in the kitchen wall to allow passing of food from the kitchen to dining area, I could see both flames and smoke very alive in the kitchen. Time to bail.

Knowing the baby was taking a nap in her room, "Di, where is Chris?"

"She's out shopping. Left to get the bus about an hour ago."

"OK, get the baby and get out. Go next door and call the fire department. NOW."

"Jack, Isabella?"

"Do as I said. I'll see to Isabella." Diana started moving, and I turned and rushed to Isabella's door, I started banging and yelling, *"Isabella, the house is on fire. Isabella the house is on fire. Nothing. But then again, I was standing almost right under the smoke detector, so how could I possibly hear past her door. But how could Isabella not hear the alarm going off right outside her room. Sleeping like the dead is one thing, but this is ridiculous.*

Whoop, whoop, whoop.

Getting no response, I was beginning to wonder if Diana could be wrong about Isabella being home. Could I be risking my life for someone who may not even be home? It would explain no response to the overpowering alarm.

Whoop, whoop, whoop.

Trying the door knob, I found the door locked. The smoke was starting to get to the hallway; the smoke was starting to get to me.

Whoop, whoop, whoop.

Remembering that it's not the flames, but the smoke that gets to you first, I was starting to get scared for my life. I could not leave not knowing if Isabella might be sleeping to her fiery death beyond the locked door. I could not leave without getting this door open to see what was or was not behind it.

I backed up a step and kicked the door, but it held. Coughing from the smoke in the hallway, I kicked again out of desperation, and I smashed in the door.

Whoop, whoop, whoop.

I rushed into the room and there on the bed looking very peaceful in sleep was the angelic Isabella. The bed was covered in dark satin sheets with Isabella resting on top of the sheets. In contrast to the sheets was her long, flowing blonde hair on matching dark satin pillow and her angelic pale skin face that looked too pale. Could she have already succumbed to the smoke? Worried for her life, I rushed to her side and discovered her breathing very lightly. She looked so beautiful in her satiny red gown that left her lightly curved shoulders bare, as well as her creamy white arms. She had such a light feminine figure with pleasant little perky breasts.

Whoop, whoop, whoop.

My eyes were starting to water from the smoke that was now following me into the room. It was getting tougher to breath from this smoke invasion into the room.

And she continued to sleep on. The room was starting to get thick with smoke and smoke detector was blaring loud enough to wake the dead and Isabella just kept sleeping on.

Whoop, whoop, whoop.

It seemed too late to even try to wake her, especially if all that racket from the smoke detector had not already awakened her.

Whoop, whoop, whoop.

So I just grabbed her up and threw her light feminine body over my shoulder using the "fireman's carry," just as I was taught in Boy Scouts. When I turned to leave the room, I discovered the smoke had gotten blindingly thick.

Whoop, whoop, whoop.

I blindly felt my way out of the bedroom and into the hallway. That placed me right under that godforsaken smoke detector again.

Whoop, whoop, whoop.

Getting that damn smoke detector behind me, I moved momentarily into the dining room.

Through the smoke it was easy to see that the kitchen was fully in flame. Both through the doorway and through the serving square, I could see the fire angrily eating everything that used to be our kitchen. It would most likely be only seconds before the hunger of the fire would break out into the living room and dining room. It would be a real good idea if I was not here when that happened.

Whoop, whoop, whoop.

With the smoke detector blaring to beat the band, I turned and felt my way past the living room wall, past the stairway up to the bedrooms, and continued out through the front door and into the clean, fresh air.

It was so bright outside that I was momentarily white blind from the sunny day. [White blind: Opposite of night blindness; one's eyesight is overwhelmed by brightness of light. One might experience it in the form of snow blindness.] Putting Isabella down onto her bare feet, I was shocked as she finally woke up, screaming in horrific pain as she suddenly and totally ignited in flame.

I heard a fireman yell, "We have a human torch here. Get that hose on her." Looking past her, I could see the firemen already had hoses attached to the fire hydrant in front of the next door neighbor's place. I saw the fireman turn the hose from the house onto Isabella.

The spray was so hard that it forcibly shoved her right into me, while the spray was putting her flame out.

Isabella burned until she became a black skull face, wearing the burned rags of her once beautiful satiny gown. She croaked, "You did this to me! You brought me out into the sunlight to burn. You did this to me!"

Totally stunned into motionlessness, I just stood there as a burned, blackened, monsteress Isabella croaked out, "You die." Her white teeth stood out in contrast to the blackened skull that made up her face and head. Those whitened teeth were now growing out fangs, a long, sharp pair of life sucking fangs.

All I could do was watch, frozen in place, frozen in fear as those pure white dealers in death, those fanged teeth moved in toward me. I could not move, as those fangs got so close as to disappear, until I felt two sharp intrusions into my neck. I could see Di playing with baby Elaine, not caring that her husband was about to die, that her husband was about to be drained of his life fluids.

I was watching Diana playing with baby Elaine as if she didn't have a care in the world. I could feel my life draining from me. I could feel ... a stiffness in my neck from falling asleep in my lounge chair with the news on. While the TV droned, "And the death toll continues to rise as three more men were found dead in North East, D.C. all within a three-block radius. ..."

My mind reeled with the memories of seeing perfectly within the dream, then my mind literally screamed the thought...*VAMPIRE. Could Isabella be a Vampire? Can our boarder be some sort of vampire?*

I need to talk with Eric. Who knows more about vampires than me? My old buddy Eric.

Chapter Nine
A Vampire Hunter is Born

"Eric, Jack's here to see you. We're leaving now. Don't you boys destroy this house while we're away." *Why Eric's wife always feels she has to guide me into Eric's home office, I will never understand. By now I know how to get to Eric's home office like I know my way to my own bedroom. For that matter, we have never damaged the house when she was away ... well, not much anyway.*

"Hey, Jack, come on in." Actually I already was walking in and finding my usual seat. I'd been in Eric's home office so often visiting with my best bud, that I needed no assistance finding my seat. I was as comfortable in Eric's office as I would be in my own home,

"Leaving?" I asked, casually pointing in the direction of the departing wife.

"They're"—referring to his wife and son—"visiting her mother. You know how her mother just loves me." Eric had once told me that his mother-in-law was a real bitch to him. He was the man who took her only loving daughter away from her (in marriage) and left her to be all alone (as her husband had run off with his under competent/oversexed secretary). Now, anytime his wife went to visit her mother, Eric stayed home out of the war zone.

Interrupting my musings, Eric asked, "Jack, you look like you have something heavy on her mind. What's up?"

"Let's play 'what if'."

"OK, shoot," Eric answered. I could tell from his tone that he was getting serious as a reaction to my seriousness in this visit. This was not going to be one of our famous Laurel and Hardy visits.

"Say I know a person who only goes out at night. When this person walks into the room, the temperature drops noticeably, but goes back to what it was when this person leaves the room...

"Sounds like a member of the walking dead. Someone very allergic to sunlight. Someone who is so deathly cold that the living can feel the room temperature change in their presence," Eric interrupted.

"There's more. This person has a voice that is painful to listen to even though everyone else raves at how beautiful her voice is. Everyone sighted, that is. When we met, she freaked at the realization that I was blind. Since then, with the help of someone else, she has been successful in evading me. I honestly don't think that this someone has any idea of the help she is rendering to ... this deadly cold creature."

At first, it sounded like you were describing a vampire, from a blind man's view, but then your description changed to that of a siren."

"And what, pray tell, is a siren?" I asked.

"I know you read *Odyssey*. Remember that Ulysses was warned about the 'song of the sirens' so he had all his men put beeswax in their ears so they could not be driven crazy by the songs of the sirens. In Greek lore, a siren is a bird woman whose song is so beautiful that it drives men to crash their ships and kill themselves. Other cultures have sirens as mermaids that again drive men crazy with their songs and their beauty. Some tales have these mermaid sirens coming up to ships and pulling men deep into the sea, to be consumed as food."

"So have you ever heard of a bloodsucking siren?" I asked.

After a thoughtful pause, Eric replied, "Nooo. Possibly a vampire with some magical ability to enthrall all those around her to see her as extremely beautiful, to have everyone bend to her will. OK, Jack, Give. Are we talking about someone ... for real?"

"Would you believe our boarder, Isabella Báthory?" I answered as seriously as possible.

Eric laughed as if I had told him the funniest joke he had ever heard.

"Eric," I called over his joviality, "Eric. I am serious."

Eric got himself under control and after a moment's introspection, he continued, "Jack, you are serious. You really believe that sweet beautiful Isabella Báthory could be a ... Vampire or a siren?"

"Eric, Di took her in while I was away at the NFB convention, right?"

"Right."

Every time I called home all I heard about was how beautiful the new boarder was and how lovely her voice was. When I got home, I met our new boarder. When she walked into the room, it got colder and when she said "hello" it almost made my ears bleed. I'm telling you, to me, her voice sounded like fingernails on a chalkboard. Di keeps going on about how she'd love to get Isabella in church, singing in our church choir. Oh yes, Eric, Di never mentioned to our new boarder that she had a blind husband. When we met, my blindness was a total shocking discovery to her."

"Shocking, you say?" Eric interrupted.

"Yeah, sounded to me like she totally freaked when she discovered I was totally blind. Di assumes that she just had never met a blind man before and did not know how to act around one. Eric, I haven't seen our boarder Isabella Báthory since. She comes and goes without my seeing her at all, ever, and I swear she's done it with Di's help. I really believe that Di does not even realize that she's helping our boarder."

"It's a shame you can't see if she has a reflection in a mirror," Eric interjected.

"Interesting you should say that. I just happen to have an extra watch here." As I spoke, I handed out my old low vision watch that I used to wear on a wide leather band. The band had two shiny gold colored shields on either side of the band that acted like mirrors. "Eric, put this on, and the next time you see Isabella Báthory, sneak a peek at the shields, and see if she appears in the shield's reflection.

Eric took the watch from me said, "You do realize that if she is a vampire using some magic to enthrall people around her, that maybe that magic takes care of the invisibility to mirrors as well?"

"I would really doubt that. Enthralling people is one thing, but enthralling inanimate objects is another."

"You have a point ... wait a minute, come on, Jack. Now you have me talking like you have a real live vampire in your home. Vampires are fictitious. They don't exist." Eric announced with strong feeling.

"So everything I have told you is my imagination. The room temperature changing as she enters and exits a room, her horrid voice which only I can hear, and her ability to control my wife to avoid seeing me again is all my imagination, right?" I demanded.

"OK, OK. I just got an idea. Isabella should be leaving for work soon. I'll just happen to be outside 'getting some fresh air' and just being neighborly I'll greet her, and as she walks away I'll see if she appears within your watch shields. OK?"

"Sounds like a plan to me. I'll just cool my jets here and wait until you return." For emphasis I made a point of sitting back, enjoying the nice, cushy seat.

"Fine, see you in a bit." With that Jack rushed out past me. The room got very quiet. A minute later, I heard the front door open and close. The quiet became entombing and then became seemingly endless. Worse, the doubt gremlins came into my mind with statements not to be ignored like, "Really. A real live Vampire? And in your home? Why not Trolls or little fairies? Vampires are creatures of fiction and you believe you have one in your house? Come on, man are you cracking up or something? Maybe Johns Hopkins failed to mention "delusions" and "going crazy" on the list of side effects of RP. I was starting to think maybe I should grab up my white cane and just slink out of there and forget I even mentioned anything to Eric, especially about Vampires.

Then I heard the front door open and close again. There was still more silence. The doubt gremlins changed their tone. *Eric did what you suckered him into, and now he is too embarrassed to even come back in his own office to tell you what a fool he feels like."* ... *"Watch your friend walk in here and order you out for making him feel so stupid.*

The doubt gremlins were interrupted by the sound of footsteps against the wooden hallway flooring, coming nearer then walking into the room. The sound of steps continued back to Eric's office executive chair without a word spoken. *Here it comes. Your bud Eric is just trying to figure out a way to tell you what a damn fool you just made of him. He's about to verbally rip your ass a new one, and you really deserve what you're about it get.*

The doubt gremlins dialogue was broken with the almost inaudible, "She has no reflection."

Jack was not sure what he had heard or possibly was not ready to believe what he had heard compared with what was preparing to hear, so he asked, "Eric, what did you say?"

"I'm still trying to believe it myself, Jack. There was no reflection of her in your damn shields." After he said that, Jack heard a rustle of movement, followed by his hand being grabbed, "Here take this damn watch back." Eric was forcing the watch back into my hand.

"Eric, please tell me what happened. Is everything alright?" I asked, concerned for my friend, and our friendship, from his tone.

After an endless silence, that was most likely only a minute or two, Eric spoke, "Only minutes after I walked out onto the front porch, Isabella came out of your place and walked out onto the sidewalk. As she passed I called out, "Hi, neighbor."

She stopped, looked my way and said, "Hi ... Eric, right?"

"That's right, Eric," I answered getting up and walking out to her. "I'm just out getting some fresh air."

"So where are your wife and son tonight?" Isabella asked me.

"They're out ... visiting with my wife's mother ..."

"You are not with them? Why? May I ask?" She asked me in such a very sexy way. Not to mention looking hot in that white, low top and short, red skirt. I was really happy my wife was not around at that moment, and all I was doing was talking with her.

"My mother-in-law and I don't agree on one thing," I told her.

Sounding very coquettish, she continued, "And what possibly could your mother-in-law and you not agree on?"

"Marrying her daughter," I answered playfully.

"Well, I can't imagine a big, handsome man like you having a disagreement with any woman." Grabbing my hand she added, "I'd love to spend my time with you, but I must go and catch the underground ... oh, you Americans call it the subway, to work." Rushing off, she called back, "Bye, neighbor, we'll have to talk again when your wife and child are away."

As she walked away, I almost forgot why I was there, as I watched her wiggle that red, short skirt down the sidewalk. But I did remember, and I did look into the watch shields you gave me and ... in the shield the sidewalk was empty. She was not to be seen. I looked again, and she was still walking down the sidewalk, but when I looked again into the shields; SHE WAS NOT THERE." Eric was getting unnervingly excited near the end of his recital.

"Eric, please settle down....," I said in a calming voice.

"Jack, don't you understand what I'm saying? She had no reflection in the mirror of the shields. Man, Jack, that bitch is a real vampire. ... I just don't believe it, but you have a real vampire living in your home."

What followed was some thoughtful silence which I did not want to break, as Eric needed the time to calm down. "OH SHIT. OF COURSE ..."

"ERIC. Please calm down," I tried again.

"Isabella Báthory. Of course. Jack, not Isabella, Elizabeth Báthory the Blood Countess. You may have the one and only Elizabeth Báthory living with you."

"Eric please, calm down and tell me, who is this Elizabeth Báthory you're going on about."

"Jack, Elizabeth Báthory, the Blood Countess, was historically a young lady who married young and then as she was getting older lost her husband in some war. Getting older, she started being obsessed with her looks and age. Well, one day while in a bad mood, she struck one of her female servants and discovered that the blood that spilled on her made her skin look more youthful, so the legend says. Well, she went crazy killing her servants left and right. Then she went about getting even more servants to kill so she could bath in their blood to keep herself looking young and beautiful."

"These blood baths really worked?" I interrupted.

"In her mind they did. Anyway, Vampire folklore has it that if you consume blood of the living while alive, when you die you become a Vampire. By the way, this historical Elizabeth Báthory was also a distant relative of the real historical Dracula. He is believed to have become a real vampire at his death because of his practice of cannibalism and the drinking of blood from his victims while he lived."

"But you said this blood countess only bathed in blood?" I interrupted.

"At first, yes. But history reports that eventually she started to drink the blood when the blood baths started to fail."

"And historically this blood countess never got caught?"

"Oh, no. Eventually she did get caught, and there was a private trial. The result was that all her helpers were put to death in the traditional way a vampire was put to death. They were staked, decapitated and then the two parts of the body were burned separately with the ashes buried in separate areas. BUT, not the blood countess."

"You're not going to tell me that this crazed mass-murderer was not put to death," I interrupted, incredulous of the possibility.

"You got it," Eric announced starting to get excited again.

"You got to be kidding me. This mass-murdering blood countess was not put to death?" I asked unbelieving.

"Remember she was a countess, and the court was made of her exceptionally influential relatives; not to mention that she had a relative who was a king. So yes, they did not put her to death. History tells that she was locked in her own bedchamber in her castle with the door sealed with only an opening large enough to slip in food. This in itself would indicate a possible fear that this blood countess might have the ability to enthrall her prison guards if a larger opening was permitted."

"So eventually she did die, right?" I asked totally enthralled in this gross history lesson.

"History reports that eventually the food trays failed to be slid back out, and this gave way to the assumption that Elizabeth Báthory, the Blood Countess, was dead. As per court order, the castle was sealed and left to decay. But what if Elizabeth Báthory after her human death, revived as a vampire? If Vampires exist, then what else is true of the vampire lore? Could the vampire Elizabeth Báthory have left the castle by transforming into a bat and flying out a window? Could she have turned herself to mist and floated out the food slot of her prison door and again floated out of her sealed castle doors?"

"So, Eric, you believe my boarder, the woman living in my house with my family is this Elizabeth Báthory, the Blood Countess, turned Vampire?"

"Jack, you supplied the tool that provided the proof. Your boarder has no reflection. In fact, now that I think back on it, her hand, when she took my hand was unusually cold, dare I say deathly cold, to the touch."

"So now what?" I asked, starting to think the worst.

81

"Well, I don't think you have to worry about your family. You don't shit where you live."

"And what does that blasphemous bit of wisdom mean?"

"As long as she is happy where she's living ... staying, she's not going to kill the residents. In other words, as long as she's happy and nobody is threatening her, she will not bring undue notice to herself by killing her landlord or anyone else in the house. ... with one possible exception."

"And who would that exception be?"

"You, my man, the blind guy. By not seeing her magical self, you may be the one *blind* man who could feasibly see past her disguise, and in not seeing, actually see her real self."

"Just great," I announced, "Just bloody great."

"I'd strongly suggest that you make a point of keeping out of her way and change your attitude so that you seem totally bluffed into thinking there is nothing strange about your never connecting with your boarder. I have another question. What do you know of her background?"

"Di did mention that she came from New Orleans. She mentioned it only because I have family that live near New Orleans."

"And before that?" Eric asked.

"There was some mention of her coming from somewhere in Europe, then moving to New Orleans. You even mentioned her travels to me, her boldness in traveling alone, from Europe .... remember?

"Yes, Diana mentioned it once while telling me all about your new boarder ..." Eric interrupted.

I don't know anything more than that, suppose I should question Di for more information on our boarder's past?"

"Definitely not. You had better start getting into the habit of living a low profile when it pertains to your boarder, the vampire."

Jack mused, out loud, "Our local news out of D.C. does seem to start out with the nightly death toll for the day. In fact, they seem to be having a murder spree in the area where Isabella Báthory works. She is adamant about not letting us go see her at work."

"I have been meaning to ask, Eric said, changing the subject, "how is it that it is too dangerous for any of us to visit her at work, but it is alright for her to work in such a dangerous area?"

"As Di explained to me, from midnight to whenever the shows end for the night, the theatre shows martial art imports. Now, not only is the area known to be risky , but the audience for such shows tend to get out of hand, even downright dodgy, so Isabella Báthory had to prove her claims that she is a Kung Fu Master and can handle any trouble that could arise within the theatre during a show. According to Di, the whole graveyard staff has to have the same training to work this particular shift. Di has mentioned that Isabella does comes home bloodied and looking like she has been in a fight or two, all too often."

"I bet she does," Eric interjected. "I bet she does."

"So what do you think I should do?"

"For now, stay out of her way. Don't let her even suspect you know anything strange about her."

"But Eric, if she's a vampire then she's a killer; she must be killing every night to continue her unnatural existence."

"So what are you going to do, sneak into her room and push a stake in her heart? Afterward, how are you going to explain a dead body in your house that *you killed*. Are you really going to tell the authorities that you killed a bloodsucker that is hundreds of years old? One who only looks to be in her twenties?"

"But if she dies won't her magic also die with her, letting everyone see who and what she really is? In Vampire lore don't vampires turn to dust once killed?"

"As to her magic, who knows? What if you're wrong about her magic dying at her death? As to her turning to dust, I'm pretty sure that is a "Buffy" invention so Buffy the Vampire Slayer and her Scooby gang did not have dead vampire issues to deal with during the shows. [Buffy's assistants/friends nicknamed her/the Scooby gang, after Scooby Doo's assistants/friends.] For now, I'd just stay out of her way. Don't do or say anything to make her suspect a thing. Just play dumb. You can do that easily enough."

"Hardy, har har," I replied. "Eric, you are telling me to just let a mass murderer, a woman who kills nightly, to continue her nightly massacres? It's not right. I feel I really have to do something. Possibly get her into the sunlight, punch a stake in her heart, something."

"Listen to you ... the blind vampire hunter."

"Blind or not, I have always been a fighter for what's right and for the women of my family. Now you're suggesting I just play dumb and let a monster killer, keep killing? Eric, that's just not me."

"It is if you wish no harm to come to your women and yourself."

"Wait, I got the answer: At least as it pertains to my family. I'll come up with some reason to have Di break the contract with our vampiric boarder. It won't rid the world of this vampire, but it will rid use of her possible dangers."

After a thoughtful pause, "Nope, I see to problems with that; one, if you succeed what's to keep your now ex-boarder for having you all as dinner? Second, I don't think you have a vampire's chance in daylight of succeeding. From what you said earlier about using Diana to keep you two apart, Isabella almost certainly has your wife enthralled to her vampiric will. No-way, would she even consider throwing Isabella out. Odds-on you'll just have one butt-ugly husband/wife fight. And what if, afterward, Diana mentions the husband/wife fight to Isabella?"

Later, when I got back home, I placed my low vision watch with the shields on the table beside the front door to be put away when I went upstairs for the night; these days I was using a talking watch.

Later that night, as my wife snored on, I just laid in bed wrestling with my thoughts. *I have a vampire living in my house. And I'm expected to do nothing. She must be killing to exist. Does that make me an accomplice to murder, to multiple murders? How can I do nothing about a vampire living ... existing in my house? Is Eric really correct that my wife, sister-in-law and the baby are safe? Make sense; she can't be staying here and killing off the residents. So what happens when she's ready to move? Could I possibly think of some way to end Isabella's existence and make it look like an accident? Jack, do you realize you are talking about killing? But she's a vampire. She's already dead. You are not killing, as long as you can make it look like you did not kill... Isabella or Elizabeth Báthory, the Blood Countess? If she is this Blood Countess, I have a crazed, mass-murdering vampire in my own house! How can I, in good conscience, allow this bloodsucking fiend to exist?*

The Blind Vampire Hunter

To say the least, I did not sleep well that night.

Chapter Ten
Death for Two Dollars

End of another shift managing the theater: *These triple movie nights do not give me a lot of time for hunting up some breakfast. I should plan on hunting tomorrow night when we have only the double billing. I guess for now I'll just lock up and wait for Metro to wake up and get me home.*

With the theatre doors locked, I turned to consider going over to IHOP; not for pancakes or waffles, but for Celeste, a fellow foreigner of this New World who figured out my true breakfast favorite, and is quite willing to be a breakfast donor, with the unspoken agreement that while I don't overfeed, she will be available for additional snack-size feedings. *She probably hopes I'll turn her or she has that foolish belief that after a number of feedings, she will turn automatically. Wrong. But who am I to dash her young, foolish dreams.*

As I pondered this, a voice in the alleyway shadows announced, "Hey, bitch! You shorted me out of two dollars. Now I'm going to get my two dollars from you one way or another."

I did not have to see the speaker. He was a big bear of a man who smelled as badly as he looked, and looked as bad as any ghoul I have ever had the misfortune to encounter. Earlier in the shift, he gave me a twenty for a two-dollar ticket, and swore when I gave him back his change, that I shorted him two dollars. He said this after he walked away and came back. When he returned to give me a hard time over the two dollars, he shoved another paying customer out of his way in his boisterous rage, all over the mythical two dollars. He almost started a fight right there in front of the ticket office with the customer he shoved.

86

The Blind Vampire Hunter

He most likely would have started a fight if a constable was not standing right there—how rare is that?

"Thought you heard the last of me I bet, bitch," the boldly obtuse voice announced from the safety of the shadows. *Who was it who said, "It's always darkest before the dawn."*

I was as coquettish as possible, and I can be very coquettish with hundreds of years of practice, "What do you have in mind, my big hunk of a man?" Taking the bait, the big lug came forth out of the shadows, with one hand over his manhood, and said, "So it's like that, bitch. Yeah, I got something for you ... if you think you can handle it."

I did not want him to come out any farther from the shadows. For one, I did not want to have to stomach that big, ugly maul of a face, and two, I wanted to give us more privacy for what was coming next. I quickly moved up to this big troll and gently forced myself against him. I slipped a hand down between his hand and his quickly bulging pants. I had years of practice at this. I moved up and inward enough to gently brush my lips against his lips which smelled like cheap beer. Using just the feathery brush of flesh on flesh, I moved up to his ear and with a gentle bite to his earlobe, I whispered, "I want you, all of you big man."

As his manhood jumped and grew at my touch, I so gently maneuvered him back into the total privacy of the shadows, the whole time moving my tongue down from his earlobe to his neck. Then, quickly, I shoved him back into the alley, pinning him against the brick wall like a fly in a web. I sunk my hungry fangs deep into the side of his neck with such force that he never got a sound off before I started feeding and bleeding him to death. *Dinner is served.* That first gush of blood forcing its way into and down my throat can be so orgasmic at times, but this pirate's blood attested to his fat build. I almost choked on the fat within his blood—almost.

Not being a great feast, I stopped feeding and moved the still bleeding body against a corner of the alleyway. I took a folded knife from my purse and slit his throat to hide my feeding bite marks. Just to give the cops something to think about, I removed his wallet and emptied the contents around, but I took both the money and the credit cards. I tossed the cards in a trashcan on the way to the underground—*subway, remember in American it is called, subway, not underground.* So much for worrying about dinner.

Later, as I was approaching the Metro station for home, two young men came out of the shadows. One announced himself, with "Hey bitch." *What is American men's fascination with female dog?.* I just kept walking, until the two walked out into the middle of the walkway, obviously to block my progress into the Metro station. The young man continued, "I said, hey, bitch. You trying to diss me woman? You better not be dissing me."

I had no choice but to stop my progress or plow through them. Movement to the side momentarily distracted me. A woman was with the two young men. *Looks like a hooker, but does not smell like a hooker. Interesting. Play this right and she could be a delightful second course.* Returning my attentions to the young men, I said, "I am sorry. I don't understand this "diss." Would you mind explaining?"

"Do I look like a word book to you, bitch?" the supposed leader of the threesome responded.

"Man, let's just have our fun with this shapely little toy," the other walkway blockade announced. "Let's just do her and walk, man. It's getting late."

To emphasize his point, he pulled out a long pocketknife, and with an audible click, a long, nasty-looking blade almost magically appeared. Before the leader could respond, I made my move...

With one hand, I put my fingers together and hardened them into a long, nailed blade. I charged forward, digging my nails into the throat of the leader just as effectively as any knife blade they had on them. His blood gushed out, making a mess of the sidewalk. I got my other hand into position and charged the second one so fast that I was out from under the crimson gush of the leader before any blood could get on me to tell a tale. Grabbing the second foe's knife-wielding hand before he could do anything more than look shocked, I bent his arm with ease, forcing the young man to cut his own throat. As I admired his life fluids draining all down the front of him, a female scream reminded me that I was dealing with a threesome, as well performing for the sake of the female. I had not completely forgotten her, though. After all, this gorish performance was for her benefit—and mine.

As the two young men sunk to the walkway, gurgling out their lives, I moved quickly up behind the young lady dressed like a hooker, who was not a hooker, and inhaled the enticing aroma of fear wafting off her so delightfully. After all, this is why the two foes died the way they did. I could now enjoy a nice adrenaline-laced dessert to my dinner, but this dessert was just not quite ready...

In my best, unnatural, demonic voice I screeched, "Are you ready to die, my dear?"

With the enticing aroma building so delightfully, she whimpered, "No, please. I'm too young to die. Please, pretty lady. Don't kill me." As she pleaded for her life, her knees started to weaken, but a well-placed hand under her armpit prevented even that small avenue of escape. She started to wet her pants. What a shame. She would ruin the delightful smell of my dinner with the disgusting aroma of piss. So, with my fangs nearly throbbing with the anticipation of this meal, I sunk my fangs into her delightfully soft neck and totally enjoyed this night's properly seasoned dessert.

Afterwards, I searched the leader for a knife. When I found one, I positioned the two foes so that it would look as if they killed each other. The scene now appeared as if one of the men killed the other for revenge for killing the girl.

On the following night, completing my paperwork was interrupted with, "Excuse me, boss, there are some dicks here and they would like to see you" My floor manager stood in front of me, nervous about interrupting my paperwork with his announcement.

"Dicks?" I asked, not familiar with the term, except being someone's name.

"Dicks, detectives, in this case, D.C. homicide. Seems we have a dead body in the alleyway next to the theatre. They would like to question you about it."

Knowing from experience that constables don't like to be kept waiting and assuming this included "Dicks," I followed my floor manager out of the office and into the theatre lobby. I found two men in cheap suits and two uniformed constables closely watching my arrival. Someone with less experience in deceiving uniformed fools would probably be feeling intimidated right now. I was not feeling anything less than confident in my coming performance. As I walked up toward the awaiting party, my floor manager discreetly separated, walking into one of the theatres, even though there were already ushers in the only theatre of the three used during the graveyard shift. As I approached, one of the suits starts with, "Miss Isabella Báthory, presently a resident in Maryland?"

"Yes, sir. And you two are?"

"Officera Dickson and Jones, presently assigned to homicide. Would you mind coming with us, just outside to the alleyway next to this theatre?" They did not have to show their badges, as they were hanging outside the breast pockets of their cheap suits.

"Lead the way, officer Dickson," I answered.

The two suits led the way with the two uniform constables following behind me. The procession went out the front door and turned left toward the alleyway, where I had dumped my dinner remains the night before. Was I worried? Of course not. These officers were just fishing for information, nothing more. Between my superior predatory night sight and my enhanced hearing during my feeding, I not only saw no one in the immediate area, but the closest heartbeats were coming from the IHOP two blocks away. No, these officers were just fishing and I was willing to bet, this fish was going to be the one who got away. As we walked out, I looked at my watch. We had a little over a half-hour before the current show ended and the next one began. I just hoped this production would be over by then.

Walking into the dark outside was no problem. When we turned the corner, a bright light caught me unprepared. I started by reflex from the sudden light attack on my eyes.

"Sorry, Miss Báthory, for not preparing you for this sight."

Bull. They set me up, wanting to test my reaction to this grotesque sight of death. I'll play their game, for now.

Acting indignant, I replied, "You walk me into this ... this horrid scene. How did you expect me to react ... to that?" I pointed in the direction of the murder scene. I did not have to look in that direction considering I was the one who staged it for the officers.

"Again I apologize, but we were informed that you might possibly know the homicide victim. Please have a look ... as distasteful as such a sight will be, please tell us if you recognize this man."

Acting the part of a frail female, I made a point of hesitating to look at the presumed (by the uniformed fools) ghastly sight. When I did look, I responded, "Sorry, I do not know this poor fellow."

"Please Miss Báthory, have another, closer look. Could his be a customer of yours? Someone you possibly sold a movie ticket to?"

I did as requested and acted as if I was getting a closer look. Then I acted as if I suddenly recognized the man. "My god, I do know this man ... that's to say I did sell him a ticket. Yes, I remember him; he claimed I shorted him some money. He almost started a fight with another customer. One of your officers interceded before the squabble turned into a fight, and also before I got a chance to look into his dispute over the shortage. I never saw him again after that. I can't say I even noticed him leave after the show."

"I have just a couple of questions. Can you tell me anything about the man you almost had the altercation with, in front of your ticket booth?

"Nooo, I really can't. Before anything really got started, one of your fine officers was present to end it before it really became an issue. I really did not give it another thought."

"Do you normally take care of the ticket sales?"

"No, Ben, the employee who normally handles the ticket booth requested to leave early because he was not feeling well. He even looked a bit poorly, so I sent him home. In his absence, I resumed handling the ticket purchases myself. I handled it myself so we would not be short handed with the ushers and bouncers in the theater, if needed. *No need to mention I could smell the illness was on Ben with my vampire senses.* I'm sure you are aware of the occasional roughnecks that the movies bring in. You don't suspect the other customer who was almost involved in the fight?"

"No. This looks like a mugging, not a fight that's gone too far. Sorry we had to call you out like this, but one of your employees recognized him as the customer that required lawful interference. We just wanted to see if you could verify this was the man and possibly give any additional information on him."

"Sorry I can't be of more help. My short interaction with this fellow did give me the impression that he had a temper problem. Possibly that had something to do with his current condition. Officer Dickson, customers for the next show may be arriving soon. May I get back to my duties? Ben is still out sick and I was not able to get a replacement for him on such short notice. I am presently running the ticket booth yet again this night."

"Yes, you may go." As I started to leave, he added, "One more thing, Miss Báthory, please take my card. Just in case something comes to mind that may be of help." As I took his card, he continued, "Thank you again for your cooperation. Sorry we had to bring you out to see this … unpleasant scene."

I could hardly say, "It was my pleasure," so I just turned and walked back into the theatre. Currently, Tim, one of the ushers, was manning the ticket booth, so I was free to see to other managerial duties. When I relieved Tim, I locked myself inside the small room and prepared to think about work. Unfortunately, seeing last night's dinner remains got me almost salivating over the possibilities for tonight's dinner. *I feel like Chinese tonight, maybe I'll go over to Little China Town for dinner. Enjoy a little China man or two.*

Chapter Eleven
Halloween

When I was sighted, I used to make the children work for their candy. On our first Halloween as man and wife, we lived in a second floor apartment with a sliding glass door and a screen door that opened out onto the balcony. We really did not have money for decorations, but that did not stop me from enjoying the holiday. It was an unusually warm Halloween, so we had the sliding glass door open, but the screen door closed. When I heard children approaching, I would let loose a wolf howl. I put on a pair of werewolf gloves with claws, and when someone knocked on the door, I would open the door just enough to get my werewolf claws out, while growling behind the door. I would open the door oh, so slowly. Then I would have fun listening to the kids scream as they ran away. One little girl was especially memorable. After letting loose a real good wolf howl, I heard a little girl, from outside on the sidewalk, exclaim, "Daddy, that was scary."

I heard her father answer, "It's alright. It's just someone being playful. I bet they have really good candy for you." When she gave a little knock on the door, I did my werewolf glove treatment, and then opened the door to the cutest little angel, who nervously announced, "Trick or treat."

For her bravery, I gave her four additional pieces of candy. With big eyes she said, "Thank you. I was almost too scared to come up here." Then she ran back down the stairs to her father, who had a big grin on his face. That was it for my wife, who exclaimed, "Enough! You scare one more innocent child, and I will take the broom to you."

Smiling, I asked, "Is there such a creature as an innocent child?"

In the following years, when we had the money, I would really prepare our place with the latest scary stuff. I would decorate like many would decorate a place for Christmas. The tradition died with the death of my eyesight.

Imagine my surprise when my wife, who for years only gave out candy, went wild decorating the place for Halloween. I was totally taken by surprise when I stepped onto the walkway leading to my single-family home and heard the sounds of chattering teeth at my feet. *The animated chattering skulls that also light up. I remember buying them. They were so cool to listen to and to watch in action.* As I walked closer to the front door, I heard, "*Go back. GOOO baaack.*" *The animated tombstone with the glowing green ghoul sitting on it. When someone got near it, the [motion activated] ghoul would turn his head, look their way, and give its warning. All so cool looking, back then.* I opened the outer door to our front foyer and when I stepped in, I heard a laughing ghost do its thing. *I thought Di had tossed that one in the trashcan since it would often cause 'trick-or-treaters' to run away, getting no candy for their efforts.*

The fun wasn't over yet. I felt the front of the inner door and, sure enough, my favorite gargoyle door knocker was in the center. Using the ring in the gargoyle's mouth made a noise like a really heavy knocker. Really cool.

I only got to enjoy the knocker once when the door opened and a very familiar voice announced, "I want to bite your neck."

"Di?" I asked in astonishment.

"Vampire Vixen Diana to you, mortal. Enter at your own risk." I could tell from the slight slur in her voice that she was wearing some type of fangs. My good Christian wife, who would only dress up as a clown or an angel for church Halloween parties, was dressed as a vampire, a Vampire Vixen, no less. I moved in to give her a kiss, which failed as she stepped back and announced, "Don't mess with the costume." I did get my hands on her shoulders enough to feel a silk fabric…*a vampire cape, it had to be.*

As I walked into the house, I said, "So tell me about this costume you're wearing, and what's the occasion? I don't recall any Halloween party at church."

While I hung my white cane by the door, she answered, "It's an off-the-shoulder peasant dress with a high-collared black vampire cape. The cape has a red interior with a black, satiny high collared exterior. Very sexy, if I do say so myself"

"And the occasion?" I asked facing her. She had always insisted that I face her, even if I couldn't see her while we talked.

"It's Halloween. I figure on having some fun this year with the trick-or-treaters." Excitement was growing in her voice, "You should see this house. I have gotten out all your old Halloween goodies and really did up the house good."

"So I heard."

Excitement began growing wild in her voice, "That's just the half of it. I have the dancing hanging skeleton hanging off the tree in the front yard."

She must have forgotten to flip the battery switch to turn that one on, or I would have heard the sound of shaking skeleton bones. "I thought you said that the hanging skeleton was too gross to put out?"

"I changed my mind. But listen. Remember that *Warning: Haunted House* sign?" Not waiting for an answer, she continued, "Isabella gave me permission to hang that in her front bedroom window."

That's nice of her, considering we are talking about the front window of OUR house. What I said was, "Why didn't you just put it in the living room window?"

"Remember that old hand-waving, animated, Dracula? It's sitting in the front window," she answered still full of excitement.

I had liked all this for Halloween back when I could see the trick-or-treaters. But now I was becoming concerned. This was sooo not Di. It was so unlike Di that it was actually scary. (I don't mean Halloween scary, I mean really scary.)

When it was time for the trick-or-treaters, I hung out in the living room and did get some fun listening to the screams coming from our front yard. There was also much excited talk from the trick-or-treaters about which was more scary, the Ghoul Tomb, the Chattering Skulls, etc.. Di really got into the vampire bit, to the point of scaring some of the kids. Later, I learned that some of the trick-or-treaters were freaking out over the candy dish which had a skeleton hand that came out and grabbed the candy grabbers. Again, I thought Di had tossed that into the trash because it was too scary for the kids. What was really scaring me was listening to Di announce, "I want to bite your neck" to the trick-or-treaters. It just was so not like her. She said it with such feeling that I wondered if she was playing for the kids or really did want to bite their necks…really freaky. This had to be the influence of our boarder, our vampire boarder.

Even Eric made the same observation the next day, "Man, I have never seen your wife look as hot as she did in that vampire outfit. And the house. My little one liked to walk my legs off. Nowhere did I see a scary house that matched yours. Joey would only walk up for some candy after I reminded him that it was his aunt and uncle's house." With a change in voice from awe to concealing, he added, "Talk about scary. You should have seen my wife. She dressed up in one of her mother's outfits, with pillow padding underneath, and a grey wig. She looked so much like her mother. Scary, really scary. Would you believe last night I even had a nightmare that I was married to my mother-in-law?" I could literally hear Eric cringe as he said the last part.

I spoke my mind, "Eric, that was so not like Di. I fear she has had some adverse reaction from having Isabella around. Last night she was playing vampire, Vampire Vixen, no less. What's next?"

"You don't think, assuming your boarder is a vampire, that she'd turn Di into a vampire? Do you?" Before I could answer, he continued, "Look, remember what I said months ago about why she would not shit where she lives? She's been with you, what, about three months, right?"

"Right…"

"And no one in your home or in the neighborhood has been hurt, right?"

"There were those two boys who disappeared last month," I answered.

"And the police suspect it was a gang-related event," Eric answered argumentatively. *"Gang related."*

"Right, and how many gangs do we have around here?" I almost yelled back in frustration. Last night was *not natural for Di, not natural at all, Di was acting like Halloween was Christmas and dressing like a sexy vampire to a bunch of kids, not natural at all.*

"Eric, could the vampire be changing my wife into a vampire, or maybe a vampire slave?"

After a thoughtful pause, Eric replied, "I have seen in movies and read in books where vampires can influence those around them. If I remember right, you had suspicions that Isabella was using Diana to keep you and her apart, right?"

"Right."

"OK, maybe if Isabella is a vampire, I say "if," then possibly Isabella is influencing your wife…"

"My god, she is…"

Interrupting me, he continued, "Is not turning your wife into a vampire, but her forcing her psyche on Di may be having an effect on your wife's character. From everything I have seen and read about vampires, this manipulation on her psyche could have a temporary effect on your wife's character, but only a temporary one."

Eric continued, "Look man, I have been keeping an eye on our Isabella Báthory." He then changed his tone to mimic Groucho Marx, "a very tough job if I say so myself." Changing back to his almost serious tone, he continued, "Outside of her working *every night*, I see nothing strange about her."

"Oh, you found nothing strange in her not appearing in my watch shields?"

"You know, I had forgotten that. I really had forgotten that.... I must have been mistaken, I must have been." I could not help but notice that such a serious Eric was also not natural. "Remember, Jack, we don't live in Buffy Land where vampires are everywhere and where you can stake a vampire and have the evidence conveniently turn to dust. You stake our Isabella Báthory and afterward you're going to have a dead body with a wooden stake in her heart and a murder one charge on your head. Face reality man, no court in the land is going to believe you staked a vampire who goes to work every night. By the way, I have been meaning to mention a little phone call I had some weeks back. One day I called the theatre where our Isabella Báthory works and asked to speak with her. I was told she only works the graveyard shift and to call back at night. So now we do know for sure that she is a working girl, and I don't mean a streetwalker. Remember Jack, if you kill Isabella Báthory in some queer act of conscience to rid the world of a vampire, you had better have some real proof that she is a real Vampire or your goose will be cooked ... and jailed."

Meanwhile, Halloween party night in Georgetown D.C.

* * * *

The one night of the year I get off from work and want to get off from work. The one night of the year I can show my true colors and not worry about it. The one night I can boldly display my fangs. My night. And Georgetown, talk about a smorgasbord. All I have to worry about is feeding on a drunk with alcohol-laced blood. On second thought, what if I do get a little tipsy–THIS IS MY NIGHT.

This is one amazing crowd. A voice interrupted my musings, "Hey beautiful. Does your mother know you're out tonight?" A man in a tux was trying to look affluent and failing. The pose just did not match the outfit, but then what I was interested in what was under the outfit, and he did look and smell healthy.

"And who, pray tell, are you?" I all but purred.

"Bond, James Bond," he answered, pulling a toy pistol from under his tuxedo jacket. "You look like a Bond girl to me."

My first meal was about to be served up. I moved in, made direct eye contact, and using my best hypnotic voice I said, "What do you do for a living?"

"I work in the mailroom of a major corporation," he almost wheezed.

Maintaining my hypnotic tone, I continued, "Well, Mr. Bond, James Bond, you are about to receive the hickey of your life. You will proudly show off in the mailroom tomorrow at work." Then I eased my fangs up to his neck and gently, smoothly put the bite on him.

He almost sunk to the ground from the orgasmic pleasure he was getting from my loving hickey. I had been prepared for such a reaction and had a hand placed under his arm, in his armpit, to hold him up. I was enjoying my dining, but I only took a small amount from him. There would be plenty of others to snack on this Halloween night. Tonight, all my crimson candy was going to be snack sized. No need to kill anyone this night. When I finished with 'James Bond', I pulled back. He looked like a man who had just lost his virginity. I realized that while I dined, as many as a couple of dozen partygoers may have observed what was going on. All would only assume we were a couple of lovers necking in plain sight, sucked into the festivities of the night. I simply left him awash in his own dreams of what had just happened. I was sure that by the next work day, he would have some wild story to go with his Halloween hickey.

I just moved on, allowing myself to be sucked into the crowd and into the festive night air. It did nag me a little that I had no idea who this "Bond, James Bond" was. I soon lost this minor annoyance within the overabundance of festive outfits. I particularly fancied the ghosts, goblins and the other vampires that were out in multitude. Eventually it did begin to bother me that out of the overabundance of fellow costumed vampires, there was not one who was a real vampire like me. "I want to bite your neck," interrupted my concern about the lack of real vampires. Suddenly, standing right at my side in the crowd of revelers was this big hunk of a vampire. Shame he was just another phony. Even within the noisy crowd I could hear his heartbeat and smell the humanity on him.

I answered coquettishly, "Right here, in the middle of this crowd?"

He grabbed my arm and pulled me through the crowd, into an alleyway. Totally away from the eyes of the crowd, he disappointed me with, "So what did you have in mind, you little vampire vixen you?"

I really thought this guy was going to be different, more commanding, more original, but then what could I expect from a guy who used that so old, over used line, "I want to bite your neck—really." So I moved in, looked deeply into his eyes, and said, "I am going to bite you in the neck."

He was so tall I had to go up on my tip-toes to get to his neck. I had to give him credit, though, he did not move or even flinch as I sunk my fangs into his neck. I thoroughly enjoyed my second snack of the night. I had a tempting thought of sharing my blood with him, truly turning this big hunk of a man into a real vampire, and I might have if he had not introduced himself with that horrid opening line. When I left the alleyway and moved back into the crowd, I looked back at the remains of my second snack. He was still alive, breathing a little hard from the lack of blood, but fine otherwise and totally in rhapsody with his thoughts. This was turning into one memorable night.

I was enjoying the night, the sights, sounds, and the smells of overexcited humans. Again my musings was interrupted by a very tall woman in a black leather outfit full of belts, buckles, and chains,

"Hey bitch. You look like my kind of meat," she said.

For a moment I thought I was face to face with a real troll. Not all trolls are ugly, just like not all humans are ugly. I took a breath of air and was assured that I smelled human under the overpowering smell of leather and perfumed soap. *Great, this over use of the female dog terminology included American women as well.* Making a point of showing off an impressive whip in her hand, she added, "I have just the thing for you, bitch."

"Surely not right here in the middle of this crowd of people?" I almost whimpered playing her role with a smile as she pointed the whipped hand at a nearby doorway, the submissive role to her dominating dominatrix. Isabella's play acting almost caused the dominatrix to slipped out of character. Regaining her composure she ordered, "Go in there and walk through the lobby without saying a word to anyone. Take the stairs up to the next floor. Stop in front of room 211, and I will let you in." Blood from a woman is just as sweet as from a man. In my pre-vampire days I only used blood from women...for my baths. Over time I did develop a feeling of strangeness from getting orgasmic while feeding off a woman. It was even stranger when my female meal would get orgasmic in my presence as a result of being feed upon. But human blood is human blood, so I followed her directions to her hotel room....

The door was slightly open, so I walked in. She was already in the room. While I could not see her as yet, I could smell her and her arousing sexual excitement. *Must have taken the elevator while I took the stairs as I was instructed.*

Once inside, I walked to the center of the room before turning to face my next snack. She was standing behind the door, so she was in position to close the door behind me. When she slid the bolt lock, she turned and let loose with the whip very impressively, snapping it loud and sharp while not endangering me by really smacking me with it.

The Blind Vampire Hunter

I moved in, making eye contact with my snack over made up eyes. As I closed in, I heard the whip slip harmlessly to the floor. As I moved in closer, I saw no reason for ruining the moment with speech. I easily sunk my fangs into her neck and went on to enjoying the meal, despite the aroma of piss leaking down the inside of her leather outfit and onto the floor. The flavoring of fear pumping through her blood system was so engrossing that I lost myself in my feeding and forgot my oath that no meal would die this night. I held her up until I had bled her to death. After I had my fill, I let her lifeless form drop to the floor, now just as dead as her whip lying next to her.

Before leaving the peaceful quiet of the room for the festive mayhem of Halloween in Georgetown, I made use of the bathroom to clean myself up. Hundreds of years old and I still could not get over no reflection in a mirror. Here I am, a beauty like no other, even if it is magically induced, and I could only enjoy it in the eyes and voices of my admirers. It is fortunate that in my current residence, the family only has mirrors in their bathrooms and their bedroom. I made a point of never going into their bedroom outside of the time I was shown the house. Of course, I have no problem never sharing a bathroom. A girl needs her privacy, doesn't she?

After making sure my vampire costume stood muster, I left the bathroom, re-entering the main room, now cluttered with a dead body.

Giving the carcass no more thought than not tripping over it while walking towards the door, after all nobody will discover this body for hours, she grinned at the thought of lobby witnesses telling the police that her last visitor was a vampire. Unbolted the door, she left meal litter behind and left the hotel to be buried alive amid the revelries once more.

The fun-filled night went on.

Eventually it got late enough that it was almost impossible to find a sober snack. I really had had my fill for the night, with only one casualty the whole night. I went back to my room in Maryland. Satiated like a tick about to burst, I slept the sleep of the dead all through All Saints daylight. The following night, I was plenty ready to go back to the quiet of the graveyard shift at the theatre. Even more so, as the first of the double billing was a Japanese horror import called Crimson Countess. The billing sounded all too familiar, I had to see it for myself.

A half hour into the movie, I walked into the closest of the two doors leading into the theatre that was showing the movie which had caught my interest. Just inside the door were Ted and Jeff, two of my usher/bouncers. Easing my way in, I told Jeff, "Jeff, take fifteen."

"Ok, boss," he whispered in a stage hushed tone. He then eased out the same way I had eased in. To Ted, I whispered, "Any problems?" I smelled the residue of smoke.

Ted whispered back, "We did have a smoker during the trailers, I gave him the option of putting it out or taking it out—he chose to put it out. No problems since."

As he spoke, I watched the big screen where a Japanese woman was bathing in blood. The camera kept moving from the bather to the funnel system with blood flowing from a corpse on a sacrificial slab, then back to the blood-bathing woman. Ted whispered, "Later in the movie the Crimson Countess gets more creative and starts using an iron maiden. The blood donors are put inside this iron maiden shaped like a naked woman. Within the front of the iron-maiden are a few well-placed spikes. As the iron maiden is closed, blood starts flowing out of the open toes and into the bath. Meanwhile, you hear these horrid screams coming from within. Really great stuff, especially when they open the iron maiden afterward, and this drained naked female falls out with all these bloody punches all over her, some in some very intimate places."

"Ted, have you seen this movie before?" I asked, wondering about how he knew so much about a scene in the movie that had not even been shown yet.

"It was in the trailer for the movie.... Really cool."

Those were the days. Just think, when I was alive, I lived for my blood baths and now I ... keep unliving with my blood meals. Those really were the days. Bathing in all that rich warm blood. It was one way to keep the Hungarian chill off one's body. I guess this movie isn't any worse, or better than any of the others like Hammer's Blood Countess, Countess Dracula and all the other movies based on my life. I have to admit, I never saw myself as a light-skinned, dark-haired Asian beauty. If they could only see me now.

The Blind Vampire Hunter

You know, it has been many-a-year since I have visited with my distant Cousin, Prince Dracula. Not a good time to go vacationing to England right now.

Ted smells like he's going to need a cold shower after this movie. Work will have to suffice for now. "Ted, walk the aisle, do your job," I ordered. As he reluctantly moved down the theatre aisle looking for the little flare of a smoker or the glint of light on an unlawful bottle, I slipped out to get back to running the place ... and the paperwork, always the paperwork. (I was thinking about Ted getting excited watching the film.) *Ted. I should talk. If I continued watching that movie, I would need to go hunting tonight, and after last night's smorgasbord, I really did not feel like hunting tonight—no, tonight I think I'll dine at IHOP.*

After I closed the graveyard shift, I still did not consider hunting for a meal this night. I just went to IHOP to dine on Celeste. Celeste, always the willing meal.

Chapter Twelve
Celeste

"No," Celeste emphatically announced from behind the locked doors of the ladies' room at IHOP. "You have been feeding on me now for months. It's time you turn me."

"Turn you?" I asked.

"Don't act like you don't know what I mean. I want you to turn me in to a vampire. I have a birthday next week. I'm getting old and losing my looks. I want you to turn me in to a Vampire before I get any older. I want you to turn me in to a vampire, **now**."

"You don't know what you are asking. You always tell me how you can't get your day started without that cup of coffee. As a Vampire you will not be able to drink or enjoy that cup of coffee anymore. What about those Apple Cinnamon Pancakes you love so much? You will no longer be able to eat those pancakes, or any other food. You will be trapped into a strict liquid protein diet. Have you considered a total diet of blood, human blood? Have you given any thought to having to survive on the blood of humans, killing your fellow human to continue your existence?"

Putting her hand to her ample belly, Celeste disputed, "I could use the weight loss of a liquid protein diet. And I would not have to continue working at this dump. I would not have to work at all. I can spend my nights hunting and just enjoying the thrill of the kill."

"Celeste, you are talking to a vampire older than I would like to say, and I'm working."

"But you don't have to work. You could be spending your nights just hunting for your meals, your free meals, I might add."

And that's the crux of the problem. She has a dangerous vampire superiority issue. This attitude could not only bring unpleasant attention to herself, but to any vampires in her area—like me. Don't I know about that, locked in my own castle until I died and was reborn; still locked in my castle, starving for blood, until I discovered how I could change my form at will and leave my castle prison.

"Honey, do you really think you can just kill for your dinner? Have you ever killed for your dinner? Have you ever done any game hunting and then dined on your kill?"

Showing signs of reluctance, she answered, "No."

At least I have her thinking. There may be hope yet. Then I said to her, "Think about it, have you ever killed anything ... let alone any *one*?"

"You feed on me without killing me," Celeste announced. "You have been feeding on me for months, so many times I can't remember, and I am still here. What about that?"

"Yes, I do feed on you occasionally, but I could not exist on these partial feedings. This is a partial feed, like a snack instead of a full meal. You can't exist on snacking. When or if you become a vampire, you will not have the maturity to control the hunger to the point of snacking on your prey. No, you will kill your prey because you will become a predator, a killer. Are you really prepared to kill? One more thing. Can you handle the guilt after your kill?"

"Possibly ..."

"Possibly nothing. Go kill someone, then come back to me and tell me you are ready to become a vampire." Knowing that Celeste was too kind-hearted to kill a fly, let alone a person, I continued, "GO, kill some person, steal their life, then come tell me you want to become a vampire."

Looking defeated, Celeste almost moaned, "I'm getting older. I don't want to get older. I don't want to get old." Then she continued defiantly, "I still will not let you feed on me again unless it is to make me a vampire," and after getting a second wind, she added, "Right here, right now."

"That's impossible even if I wanted to. Becoming a vampire takes time and must be at the right place. You do realize you are asking me to kill you. You do realize you have to die to become a vampire." *Not totally true, I have heard of Living Vampires, Celeste does not have to know that.* "Celeste, dear, we would need a place where you can die and be reborn. The process of dying and becoming reborn can take minutes, hours, or days. We would need a proper, quiet place where your dead body can rest in peace until you re-awaken as a vampire. This just cannot be done here within a busy ladies' toiletry."

Her eyes widened when I said 'kill here.' She had not considered being killed. Push the point. She is not ready to die. "Are you ready for me to kill you, to feed on you to the point of permanently taking your life? Do you really want me to kill you, dear Celeste?" I emphasized my point by extending my fangs in her sight. Celeste had seen my fangs before, but she had never seen them as instruments of her death. She visibly flinched at their appearance.

"There is one more point about which you need to consider. Becoming an immortal Ghoul."

"A what?" Celeste asked, doubt sneaking into her voice.

"A Ghoul. A grave-robbing eater of the dead. A disgusting brainless creature shunned by even the worst of the creatures of the night. A creature of decay that exists on the decaying flesh of the dead. There is nothing lower than a ghoul and, for some unknown reason, sometimes a "turning' goes wrong and the newly dead is not reborn as a vampire, but is reborn as a disgusting, decaying, creature ruled by a decaying brain that only wants one thing, to eat the dead. Do you really want to take the chance of spending immortality as a disgusting decaying brainless ghoul? Personally I would not like to see that happen to you."

Sounding a little defeated, she asked, "But if that did happen to me, wouldn't you end my ghoulish existence?"

Making a point of looking and sounding sad, I answered, "I really don't think I could. I would have to touch your repulsive form long enough to end your existence. I really don't think I could." Sadly shaking my head, I added, "No I really could not touch you, let alone end your existence."

That's giving her something to think about.

I decided to put the last nail in the coffin, "There is always the possibility that something could go wrong and you will just die. Remember, while I know the procedure, which I learned by word of mouth, I have never seen, let alone performed, a 'turning'. There really is a greater chance that something will go wrong, than that the turning will go right."

Sounding childishly defeated, Celeste replied, "Please leave. No snack tonight, just leave."

Feeling relieved, despite my lack of a snack size meal, I walked over to the ladies' toiletry door, unlocked it, and quietly left for the subway. No meal tonight.

Chapter Thirteen
Dr. Who

Meanwhile, in the life of a future blind vampire hunter. Years ago when I changed my medical plan to a new HMO, I needed to pick a general practitioner, also called a primary care doctor. I looked down the list and saw *Dr. Who*. How could a sci-fi nerd like me pass that up? Pass up telling my nerd friends that my doctor is Dr. Who? No way.

I became a little hesitant when I read that the doctor was a female, but I also read that she spent some time working at John Hopkins, so I choose her as my doctor. This pretty little Asian has been my doctor for about five years now. I only had to drop my pants for her once during that time. It was all very professional and no problem, as she is not a woman, she's my doctor—my Dr. Who.

Today I had a follow up on the growth which had been removed. It had been sent to the lab to be tested for cancer.

I followed the usual procedure. After paying my co-pay, I sat out in the waiting area to be called in to see the doctor. This time when the nurse called me, instead of following her with my white cane, I asked if I could take her shoulder so that she could lead me into the examination room, easier being led then feeling my way behind her, possible tripping her with the white cane if I get too close. She complied.

After helping me up onto an examining table, she went about taking my temperature and my pulse. Both were fine.

After a reasonable time waiting, Dr. Who knocked on the door and let herself in. As she walked in, she asked the usual, "So, how are you doing?" Then she sat down.

I could not pass it up and answered, "Well, I have gone totally blind."

It sounded as if she almost missed sitting on the chair with that come back.

Then she questioned, "Mr. Poisner, you serious?"

"Yes, ma'am. Since the last time I saw you I went from legally blind to totally blind. I had been warned for years that it could happen, that a sudden activity of the RP could have me going to bed sighted and waking up totally blind. Well that's what happened to me. I woke up one morning seeing nothing, nothing but grayness."

"You say 'grayness' and not blackness?" My Dr. Who asked

"Seems strange even to me, but everything and the only thing I see is grayness. I have gotten so that I can tell if I am in a lit room or a dark room from the degree of grayness. I can tell the difference from being out in the sun compared to being out during the night. But that is all I can *see*."

"How are you copping with this change?"

"OK. I am still adjusting. For example, I had my wife drive me to my appointment instead of coming by myself using Metro. I figure, given time, I will regain my confidence to travel outside the home by myself again someday. Of course I miss even the half-assed eyesight I had for so many years."

"That's understandable. You sound in good spirits, under the circumstances. Just the same, if you feel like some time at mental health would help you right now or even later just let me know and I will set you up with a referral. If you should suddenly find yourself feeling suicidal over your loss of sight you can call Mental Health at anytime day or night and instantly get an appointment with no referral needed."

"Thanks doc, but I really am doing alright." I was tempted to add *except for the Vampire living under my roof.* I didn't. I grinned at the thought of her possible reaction if I had done so. *Do they keep those special white coats with the extra-long sleeves handy around here?*

"Something funny, Mr. Poisner?"

"Sorry, private joke."

"Mr. Poisner, you will be relieved to know the mole that was removed was benign. Please take off your shirt. I will have a look at your back. See how everything is looking."

So I removed my t-shirt and listened to her coming around behind me. She felt the area where the mole had been removed and proclaimed, "Looks good. Hardly can tell where the mole was removed. Just remember to have your wife occasionally check for any signs of the mole returning. From what I have seen, I doubt that will be a problem."

She walked back to her chair, most likely to make some notes, "As to your loss of eyesight. Remember you can call mental health day or night and get help immediately."

"Really, it's no sweat doc. I'm not getting around outside the house on my own as I used to, but I believe in time even that will change as I regain my confidence in being totally blind as I did when I was legally blind. Would you mind helping me find my way out to the waiting area to my wife?"

Going home, my wife was quite relieved at the confident report from my doctor, as some folks at church and at work had been feeding her horror stories of reoccurring melanoma.

Chapter Fourteen
The Celeste Problem

Celeste's attitude, when I was last with her, troubled me. Who's to say an unhappy Celeste would not get mouthy about knowing a vampire? How do I know she wouldn't give me up in the dejected state I left her in?

I have too good a thing going here to lose it over a little malcontent from a waitress. Celeste is going to have to be taken care of. *Tonight. The theatre has only a single movie scheduled, so I will have plenty of time after closing to see to Celeste's needs. Celeste, tonight is your night.*

Sitting at my usual table at IHOP, Celeste approached looking as if I was the last person on Earth she wanted to see. I just kept a smile on my face as she continued to approach with an air of defiance. *Yes, Celeste, tonight is going to be your night.*

Celeste was the first to speak. "You have your nerve showing up here. Don't expect to get the usual. That feed fountain is closed."

Interrupting her tirade, I said, "Celeste, hon, I decided tonight is your night. Go tell your boss you are going out for a smoke break. Tell him to take this job and shove it, if you prefer. While you are doing this, I will be leaving and going down the street to the deserted, unused warehouse down the block. You know the one I mean?"

With a notable change in attitude of excitement, she replied, "Yes, yes I know the place."

Interrupting her youthful display of enthusiasm, I continued, "There your life is about to change forever. There you will get 'turned'."

Looking like a little kid on Christmas morning, Celeste announced, "Really? Oh thank you, thank you...."

111

Again, I interrupted her display of merriment, but I was happy to note the lack of interest by the few diners within sight or hearing, "Celeste, dear, calm down. You don't want to raise anybody's suspicions. Get yourself under control and do as I say, and before dawn you will be totally changed."

Celeste made a notable effort to replace her childlike display of merriment to her usual, careless "every night is just the same boring night as the night before" attitude.

When Celeste left to follow my instructions, I got up and left.

I hadn't been standing within the shadow of the warehouse for long, when a youthful Celeste could be seen running toward my position. She reeked of innocent enthusiasm. She was hardly being covert with her out-of-control emotions. I listened closely around the area. I could hear no heart beats nearby that were human. Luckily no one was around to observe Celeste's self-indulgent display.

On her approach, she looked at me, then at the chained and pad-locked warehouse door and announced, "We're not getting in that way."

"No, we are not. While I could easily break either the chain or the lock, someone might walk by and observe such evidence of intrusion into the warehouse. We don't want to be interrupted on this very special night." Forcing a smile to fit Celeste's festive mood, I continued, "We will go around the corner and find a way in from the side of the building. A way in where any damage we create will not be seen by anyone but some alley rats."

"Rats. I hate rats," she nervously announced, looking around for the little rodents.

With authority I pronounced, "Fear not. You're with me. No rats will be bothering us this night."

Without being told, Celeste followed her into the alley beside the warehouse. There Isabella, only with the aid of her predatory night sight, found two windows. She chose the window deepest into the alleyway. For one thing, she did not even have to break the window to unlock it. For effect, she forced the window open without bothering to unlock it, to display the amazing strength Celeste will be inheriting after her "turning." This feat of strength was not lost on Celeste, who did not even try to hide her excitement about the possibilities that could soon be hers.

Isabella stepped through the open window first, so she could assist Celeste, the woman of the hour, safely inside. This also put Isabella in position to help Celeste into the darkened structure, which she did find to be a problem.

Celeste's smock got caught on the broken window lock. It was easy for the vampire to free her special human being's outfit and continue to assist the woman of the hour into the abandoned warehouse. With her safely inside, the vampire led her further into the decomposing room, which had given way to time and neglect.

Once inside, the vampire couldn't help smell her special friend's growing excitement, and also nervousness. "I can't see in here. I can see a little light in the alleyway, but here inside this building I can't see my hand in front of my face." Celeste was comically waving her hand before her face for emphasis, but for the vampire with her predatory night sight, seeing was not a problem.

"Here, put out your hand, and I will be your guide." She did as she was told, so the vampire took her hand and pulled her near. As she looked around the place, it looked like a prime candidate for the wrecking ball; rubble was all around. There was a stairway in the middle of the large room, a stairway that went nowhere. After a few steps upward, it just did not exist anymore. From the lack of human rubble, the vampire guessed that even the homeless had abandoned this building a long time ago.

At first the vampire did not see the perfect spot for tonight's festivities, so the two ladies were going to have to do some exploring. Before moving, Isabella instructed, "Celeste, the flooring is full of rubble, so follow my lead, but pick your feet up, as we will have to travel over some boards and fallen pieces of ceiling tiles. It's going to be rough going, but remember I have your hand and will not let you fall."

"Alright," she almost squeaked out, nervously.

The two walked in the general direction of the stairway with the idea of checking out a darker area just a little behind the stairway to nowhere. They had only gone a couple of feet when Celeste tripped over some bit of ceiling rubble on the floor, but the vampire prevented her from falling without a problem. "Celeste, dear, please pick up your feet and watch your step."

"Yes Isabella." With each step, Celeste seemed to be getting more nervous. *Is she having second thoughts? Too late for that now.*

Eventually the two ladies, one young and the over very old but not showing it made it to the their destination, the darkened area in the middle of the building of rubble Celeste only tripping two more times while on their short journey. As Isabella suspected, the darkened area of interest was a large hole in the floor. Perhaps this hole had been an elevator or some large piece of equipment that was large enough to take up two or three floors, as even Isabella with her vampire night sight could not see the bottom of the large hole. While Isabella continued holding Celeste's hand, she kicked a piece of wood into the hole and listened for it to hit bottom. It did, eventually. From the sound, it was at least two floors down, possibly three. With her vampire hearing she noted that the fallen wood had scared up a large number of squealing mice, rats and other little urban insectoid predators. *This is the place.*

"So, Celeste, are you ready for the big change?"

"Oh, yes..." She sounded like a little girl who had been asked by her parents if she was ready to go downstairs and see what Santa had brought her.

Isabella gently pulled Celeste to herself. She lovingly embracing the girl in her arms, pinning her arms to her sides. She couldn't help getting hungry at the thought of what was coming next. Celeste did not fight, but her adrenaline was starting to pulsate through her system in anticipation of what was about to come. After all, she was about to finally get what she had been requesting for some time. She was about to get hers.

As she slowly sunk her fangs into Celeste's soft creamy neck, the adrenaline-spiced blood was almost orgasmic. In Celeste's eagerness to finally get what she had always wanted, she provided her vampire with the best meal she had ever provided. And Isabella drank on, and on...

As she continued to engorge herself on Celeste, she could sense Celeste's realization that her vampire was overfeeding, that Isabella was killing her. As Celeste tried to struggle free, fear of impending death let loose a fresh gush of adrenaline into Celeste's blood stream. This was icing on the cake for the vampire who just kept on feeding...

Celeste soon realized that her death was near. Her self-preservation system kicked in, despite knowing that this was part of "the turning," despite the knowledge that this was just what she wanted, she tried mightily to get free. Even with her adrenaline rushing extra strongly throughout her system, she was no match for the vampire's supernatural strength. Trying to wrestle free of Isabella was like trying to wrestle free of a grizzly bear, and just as futile. Eventually, from lack of blood getting to the brain, Celeste died.

The meal was over. Isabella just tossed the ragdoll remains of Celeste into the hole. Again, this set off a startled squeal of mice and rats. Being in no hurry to leave, she presently stood listening for a while and was rewarded with the tiny munching sounds of lots of very hungry little teeth, all gnawing away at the dead remains of dear Celeste.

"I am going to miss you, girl, especially after that last meal you just gave me."

When she left, Isabella made a point of pulling the window back down, just in case the local constables started searching the alleyway for a missing Celeste. Would there even be a search if she had told her boss what to do with the job. Tomorrow or the next night she would have to go back to IHOP just to make an appearance so that her lack of use of the restaurant couldn't be tied to Celeste's disappearance in any way.

Most likely, if a search was performed for a missing Celeste, it would not be for days. Eventually, if the local constables think to investigate the warehouse, the mice and rats of DC will have consumed the evidence of Celeste's death. I should have busted out her teeth, just in case Celeste's skeleton was found ... oh, well.

Isabella, you are giving the dumb arm of the law too much credit.

Two nights later with only a single showing that night and plenty of time to kill before metro opened for morning service, I tossed some paperwork into an attache case and made an appearance at IHOP. I sat down and seemed to enjoy some coffee while playing catch-up with the paperwork.

I made a point of sitting at my usual table and started digging out the paperwork while waiting to be served. While I was still getting the night's work organized, a pretty youthful redhead interrupted me, "So what will it be tonight?" I noted her name plate read "Mary."

Looking up, I faked surprise at not seeing Celeste and asked, "Celeste has the night off?"

"You could say that. She quit two nights ago. Told the manager she was tired of working this 'cheap dive' and walked out..."

Good going, Celeste.

"No one was really surprised. She'd been acting a bit unhappy here lately, almost like she was working something on the side. Some think she might have found a 'sugar daddy.' Although, if she found a 'sugar daddy,' it wasn't someone she met here. We just don't get customers like that around here. You know, very rich and all."

"'Sugar daddy', what is 'sugar daddy'?" I did not have to act interested, as I really had not heard this term before.

"A 'sugar daddy' is usually a rich guy who is rich enough to set up a woman on the side. He may set her up with her own apartment or house. He may give her loads of expensive gifts and/or money to keep her satisfied. I guess the reverse could be true. That would be a 'sugar momma' would it not?" The joke was dying faster than her last dinner.

"Excuse me, Mary, just coffee, black."

"Yes, of course," and she left.

Celeste quit. How sweet that is. It might be days before anyone notices her disappearance. Having no family, is it possible that Celeste may never become a police matter? Meanwhile, just two blocks away the mice and the rats of D.C. eat away at the evidence. How nice is that?

I wonder if I should play Mary and see if she might be a candidate to replace Celeste for quick, small meals. I should give Celeste's disappearance some time before even trying something like that.

Well, Celeste, if no one else misses you, I will miss you ... as a quick snack that is. I should get some paperwork done, so later I will have some time to find someone to dine on tonight.

Chapter Fifteen
Bad Night at the Theatre

Busy yet again with the endless theatre paperwork, just wishing for some distraction...

Ted, one of the ushers stormed in. When Isabella saw his expression, she thought, *Girl, be careful what you wish for.* Ted announced with youthful excitement, "Sorry, boss. We got trouble in the theatre."

"What trouble?" she deliberately asked in a composed tone in hopes of calming down all that youthful exuberance.

"FIGHT."

"Calm down. Are you telling me that you and Jeff can't handle it..."

"Boss, it's a mob scene, and a little girl has been knocked out cold."

I rose from my seat, and asked, "Has any one called 911 for constables and ambulance?"

"Constables?" the usher asked.

"Police. Have the police and ambulance been called for?"

"Yes, Ben is using the phone in the ticket room as we speak."

As he answered, I was already rushing out from behind my desk preparing to get into the action. *What is a little girl doing in that theatre watching what is basically an "X-rated" movie?*

Ted led the way out into the theatre lobby, but I passed him and left him and the snack counter behind me. The theatre door was open, so I could see that there was a true mob scene in the theatre. The projectionist had already stopped the movie and turned on the ceiling lights. *Good going, Mark.*

When I rushed in, it appeared that five men were facing off against the rest of the audience; the fists were already flying. The two ushers, totally outnumbered, were staying out of it. Both looked guilty upon Isabella's entrance. *I'll have to commend those two on their wisdom in not getting involved in this one.*

On the other side of this mayhem of anger-crazed men, was a crying woman, hugging and rocking a child who looked dead. With effort, Isabella was able to sort out the noise and hear the little heart beat of the child. Apparently the little rag doll was just knocked out cold. She wished she could inform the grieving mother of the facts. The grieving mother looked like she really believed her daughter to be dead. Right now though, she had a bigger problem to solve.

Facing the crowd, Isabella threw out her best enthrall voice and announced, "Cease and desist!" On the ceasing of hostile blows, Isabella ordered, "Separate!" The five moved to the left, and the rest of the mob moved to the right. The whole mob looked confused, possibly wondering why they were obeying this strange woman with such controlling authority. Isabella was about to ask about the child when the local police stormed in. One of the men in blue demanded, "What's going on here?"

His question set off a mayhem of angry cries trying to talk over each other, and no one was successful.

"Quiet!" Isabella ordered and the room died in silence. As Isabella started to talk to Jeff, the main usher, sirens could be heard getting close. *The ambulance, I hope.* "Jeff what happened here?"

"These gentlemen and that woman sitting over there..." He pointed to the five fighters that had formed a group and a woman sitting nearby. Apparently they succeeded in sneaking in a large purse full of pony bottles. As they got drunk on the pony bottles, they began tossing the bottles at the movie screen. "These gentlemen and that mother and child" pointing to the larger group and the bereaved mother, "had that little girl with them. Before we could stop the bottle throwing, one of the bottles bounced off the screen and hit that little girl. Then all hell broke out."

The leader of the mob facing off against the five announced, "They hurt my little girl. Look, she's out cold. I want those men arrested, RIGHT NOW."

That triggered another shouting match which Isabella ended with a sharp, commanding, "Quiet!"

One of the policemen looked at Isabella as if he wished he had her talent to handle mobs. Just then the EMS rushed in with stretcher between them. They saw the woman holding the limp child and rushed over to work on her.

The police started cuffing the five, with the help of additional police who had arrived right behind the EMS. The EMS finished preparing the little girl for transport to the local hospital. Isabella announced in a voice loud enough to be heard within the projection booth overhead, "Those not assisting the police or the EMS please find a seat. Once the emergency personnel are gone, we will continue the movie."

As the little girl was being carried out on the stretcher, the lead EMS stopped to tell Isabella, "The child has a sizable bump on her head. She is already showing signs of coming around, so I believe she will be alright." Following the EMS was the tear-stained mother, with the father taking up the rear. Isabella stopped him for a moment. "Please feel free to return for a movie on us. Perhaps I might suggest you leave your daughter at home or bring her to an appropriate family movie during the day." If looks could kill, Isabella would be dead. With a quick glance in the direction of the police, she could see him fighting the temptation to respond verbally. Instead, he continued out without any verbal retort.

With the ambulance sirens disappearing in the distance, the theater lights went out and the movie continued. Back in the office, Isabella continued the tedious paperwork. Until...

Again she was interrupted with, "Boss, we have a blade runner." (Blade runner meaning a crazy with a knife.)

Rushing past Ben, into the theatre for the second time this night, Isabella found the movie stopped and the lights on, again. A man was standing off the rest of the moviegoers off with a good-sized folded knife, blade out and bloody. *Just great, whose blood is that?* Looking around, she took note of another movie viewer in his undershirt with an outer shirt wrapped around his hand. She looked back at Jeff, and asked, "Has 911 been called?"

"Yes, boss."

The crazy with the knife started yelling, "That knife expert doesn't know a knife from a toothpick."

In her best calming voice, Isabella asked, "What knife expert do you refer to?"

"Why that joker of a so-called knife expert in the movie, that's who. I'm far better than that joker on his best day."

Walking closer to the blade runner, she stated, "Sir, I'd be willing to bet you're right. I personally have not seen this movie, so I could not truly say. You do realize this is only a movie..."

"A movie I paid $4 to see ... this farce."

"Sir, if you put that knife away and walk out with me, I will gladly give you back your money and give you a free ticket to another movie of your choice."

He replied with a challenge as if he had not heard her words, "I'd like to see you remove this little knife from me."

She could easily make a move on the blade runner except that Jeff was standing in the way. *What is he doing, playing hero to a crazy with a knife? I'm going to have to have a word with him, later.* For now, Isabella ordered, "Jeff, back off."

Obeying, Jeff started moving backward, not taking his eyes off the crazy, just in case the blade runner decided to strike ... and the crazy man with the blade did.

With Jeff still in Isabella's way, the blade runner charged forward with his knife arm fully extended, heading right for Jeff's chest. Just as the knife blade pierced Jeff's shirt, it came to a deadly and complete stop.

Isabella put such a vise grip on the blade runner's wrist, that the crushing of bones might have been heard if it wasn't for the blade runner screaming in pain, a scream that preceded the snapping of his bones.

When the blade runner's knife fell to the floor, Isabella ordered, "Jeff, get the knife."

Jeff did as he was ordered and sirens could be heard rushing to the theatre for the second time this night.

While one of the EMS cleaned up and bandaged the movie viewer with the slight cut to the hand, another saw to splinting the crushed remains of the blade runner's wrist. The police then escorted the blade runner to the local hospital by ambulance. Before leaving, one of the officers made it clear that they were not happy with the bone-crushing injury to their prisoner.

Isabella just answered sheepishly, "I guess I just don't know my own strength." The show continued while Isabella buried herself in her office to dig into the paperwork, always the paperwork.

The way this night is going, I am so pleased that this is a single movie billing night.

After closing down the theatre for the night, it was time to go hunting, possibly because of the sight of blood on the knife or the smell of the blood-soaked hand, it did not matter. What mattered was that it made this girl hungrier than usual for fresh blood, so the hunt was on.

Isabella was starving for a nice fresh dinner. Maybe tonight she'd go bar hopping and with luck find a meal that would take her home for dinner. In other words, she could not bring her dinner to her domicile, her human-filled home, but to her dinner's home and the place of his/her demise. This was definitely not a snack night. Tonight someone was going to die for her dinner. Within her dinner's domicile this could be more casual, relaxing dining. If she played her cards right she could leave her dinner remains behind without any clues as to who the killer was.

Chapter Sixteen
Christmas

It's Christmas Eve and I have no choice but to take the night off, the theatre is closed. If only I could have gotten a chance to talk to management. I bet if *we would have opened for business on Christmas, we would have had enough seasonal losers to fill this theatre even on this so-called holy night. Management had put out a memo a week before closing and then left town for the holidays.*

Isabella pondered. *With the Poisner house all decked out for the holidays, and all the excitement of this being baby Elian's first Christmas, staying home was not an option. Maybe I'll go bar hopping in D.C. in an area that's new to me, go exploring for dinner. Very possibly I can find some lonesome meal that will take me to his place for some nice quiet holiday dining. I don't mean a dinner of spiced eggnog and turkey, unless it's a human turkey.*

When she left her room, it only proved her point. The living room and dining room were gaudy with flashing and non-flashing Christmas lights, bright, shiny Christmas decorations, and cheerful foolery of all sorts.

When she saw that constantly moving Santa Claus doll again in the window, it made her stomach turn. *I can't say which is, worse that constantly moving Santa doll, or the moving doll of Dracula they had in the window for Halloween.*

Diana, seeing Isabella, interrupted her play with Elaine and called out, "Isabella, you're just in time to say good-night to our little bundle of joy."

122

"Good night Elaine, pleasant dreams." When she heard Isabella's voice, Elaine, as always, responded with wailing. *I should have known better. Maybe I could give that "little bundle of joy' a nice crib death for Christmas. Put her and her constant screaming at the sound of my voice out of my misery. Hmmm.*

"Yep, time for bed. She must be getting over tired." As Diana happily rushed crying baby Elaine to bed saying something to her about getting to bed so Santa can come, Isabella pondered that her magic must not work on such a young mind. Seeing that Jack was now the lone occupant of the couch, she noted that Jack looked self absorbed. *Oh, yes. This is his first Christmas without eyesight. The least said to him the better. I'll just sneak out while Diana is busy with the baby.*

Once outside, she thought, *I can't get over how warm a Christmas it is, not unlike New Orleans. When I relocated north, I was so looking forward to seeing a white Christmas again. I haven't seen a white Christmas since my time in Europe. Well, I'll go find some interesting Christmas dining.*

As she started heading for the metro, she saw Eric. *I guess I'm going to have to be neighborly.*

"Hi, Isabella. Merry Christmas," Eric called out from the front steps of his place.

He sounds drunk ... already. I looked past Eric into the living room window. *No Christmas tree, no Christmas decorations at all ... odd.* "Eric, where's your wife and little boy?"

"Wife and my boy are with my mother-in-law, or should I say mother-*out*-law." With a laugh at his own bad joke, he continued, "Ever since we got married, my wife goes to her mother's place to spend Christmas Eve sleeping in her old room so she can spend Christmas morning, not to mention the rest of the day, with her mother. Of course I'm not invited."

"Yes, I remember you mentioning that you and your mother-in-law don't get along. She hates you for taking her only daughter from her in marriage, correct?"

Shaking his head drunkenly, Eric answered, "You got it. ..."

"But for Christmas? Have you even tried to reconcile with your mother-in-law?"

"For my baby boy's first Christmas, I suggested to my sweet old mother-in-law that, for the baby's sake, we should bury the hatchet. You know what she said?"

"Can't imagine."

"She asked if I had a hatchet so she could bury it into my head." Eric paused to let that sink in.

Sounds like my type of woman. She fought off a grin.

"Please excuse my manners. Would you like some heavily spiced eggnog?" He showed off the more than half empty gallon plastic jug with the label "EGGNOG' clearly in view. Eric continued proudly, "I spiced it myself, I did."

"No, thanks. It's a little early for "spiced' drinks for me," she answered.

"Ah, yes, you don't drink ... liquor." Eric drunkenly snickered.

Now what did he mean by that?

"So Miss Isabella Báthory. Who do you plan on drinking tonight?" Eric drunkenly asked proudly puffing out his chest, "Who do you plan on drinking tonight?"

She rushed up to Eric faster than any human possibly could, and faster than anyone could have seen. Isabella planted her face in front of Eric's face, made eye-to-blood-shot-eye contact with him, and enthralled him. "Eric, you are too drunk to remember this conversation. You did not see me tonight. Now go to sleep." No sooner said than done. Eric collapsed on the stoop and started snoring. Thinking that his poor wife must be sleeping quieter tonight, Isabella picked up Eric as if he was a child and carried him into the house. She walked around the living room couch and dumped him on it. The jug of eggnog never left his hand. She removed it from his grasp and placed it on the coffee table. Looking at the jug she noted that not only did the sickly light yellow contents look totally unappetizing, but she could not begin to see how she could have even gotten the dreadful smelling liquid past her nose. She could not decide what was worse, the smell of eggs or the horrid smell of the cheap liquor within.

Looking back at him sleeping, she thought, *Eric, I really hope I heard you wrong. Heard you wrong twice, but it's unlikely*. Out loud she said, "It's a good thing you're Jack's best friend, or this night you would be my first Christmas dinner after that remark you made. Despite being Jack's best friend, you just may have become a problem that I will have to deal with." That thought brought a slight pang of regret and loss over dear Celeste. It turned out that Celeste wasn't even missed enough to be a problem for the police. It would seem that I was the only one to miss sweet-tasting Celeste.

Just then Eric moved his head to the side displaying his neck, almost daring her to take a bite out of him. It was tempting, but Eric was not worth the chance of losing her happy day respite. Besides, it was too early for such a heavily-drunken dinner. She left to the unpleasant reverberation of Eric's snoring.

Once down in D.C., it was no problem finding a pub open for the holidays. With her predatory heightened sense of smell, all she had to do was follow her nose. With each block she left behind, the scent of drunken sweat and strong liquor of a local pub in full action got stronger until she came within glowing lights that announced "Budweiser" and "Mil..." (Only part of that sign was lit). It was interesting that the bar's name ... American Girl ... was not lit up. While it sounded busy, it did not sound busy with Christmas joviality. Just the place to find a lonesome, fresh Christmas dinner.

Noting how deadly quiet the rest of the block was, she crossed the street and walked in. The atmosphere of stale cigarette smoke made the place look like a London fog had floated in. If the smell of stale cigarettes wasn't bad enough, add to the olfactory system the invasions of smells of various liquors fighting among themselves, and then mix in the stink of unwashed bodies, and morning applied deodorant that failed to survive the night.

While fairly busy, the place was as quiet as a graveyard except for the juke box playing some sad song she'd never heard before and would have been happy not to be listening to now. This was definitely the "Bah, Humbug" crowd. This was such a group of losers that finding a nice Christmas dinner was going to be like hunting for virgins in a nunnery. That brought back memories of joy both fitting the Christmas night, while not fitting a Christmas night. Hungry to the point of nearly starving to death after escaping my castle prison, I stumbled onto a convent full of nuns, an assembly full of virgin women, a feast fit for a starving vampire. Only later did I ponder how my helpers failed to find such a cache of virgin blood for my baths, but then, I only found this secluded, out-of-the-way structure by misfortune. What a night of screams and sweet crimson meals that night was.

She forced her mind back to the present. Looking around, it appeared that she had her pick of two biker bums with their own biker broad, or at another table there were three street types who hardly looked old enough to be in a bar. At another table was a suit with his tie hanging low and the top two buttons of his shirt undone. He was displaying a tasty neck. Being along, he was a good possibility, but being the suit type, he probably had a nice apartment—possibly too nice, one with a doorman who could give police a description of his last guest after she left her dinner remains behind. She turned her attention on the other possibilities. There were two men at the bar who looked interesting. Both looked the type to be easily enticed sexually, then she could toss in a little last minute fear of death for the spicing. In the corner was a worn out looking whore who looked as if she was more into drinking than looking for a john. "John" reminded her of her short career as a street walker who was paid in blood. The gothic outfits she used to dress in were so cliché. But the hip, edgy outfits had made it easy to open negotiations for sex for blood payments. Eventually, she even had returning customers who did not even require her to "put out" for their blood. They just got off by becoming blood donors, but one does get tired of only snacking and not enjoying the fill of a full meal.

It was time to reel in that next full meal. She decided to take a seat at the bar and see who took the bait first.

"What's your poison?" a tired bartender asked.

"Poison?" Isabella asked.

"What do you want to drink?" the bartender restated annoyingly.

"Bloody Mary." She would not be drinking it, but if things went well, she would not be around long enough for the untouched drink to be an issue.

Just after the bar tender delivered her fake-blood concoction, she heard, "Can I buy you a drink?" When she turned toward the voice, it was the suit from the table. *It didn't take long for him to come over from his table. I would have bet one of the other men sitting at the bar drinking would have been the first to take the bait.*

"I have one thank you." *Let's not look to eager, play hard to get–a little.*

"Yes, I see." Sitting down next to her, he continued, "Let me introduce myself. I'm Phil Bowman. Seller of kitchen appliances. I have been here for some time now, and let's face it. This place is a real dump."

Isabella noted the unfavorable reaction of the comment from the barman working in earshot. He could not have disagreed too much as he continued cleaning drinking glasses with an unsavory looking rag, "I have much better wine at home than this guy sells. Let's go to my place, where we can enjoy a nice bottle of wine and a warm fireplace..."

When he said that, he placed his hand on hers and added, "Your hand is cold. You could use a nice warm fireplace. I bet you're from the south and not used to this northern weather, even though it is unusually warm right now. Am I right?"

I'll just smile a little and look back at the drink I'm not drinking. She deliberately hesitated in answering. *Let's play with this mouse a little.*

"I have some real music at my place, from Sinatra to Meatloaf."

She just smiled to give him a feeling of a possible victory to come.

"Look, lady, I have a bed that not only heats but vibrates and can move like a real water bed. What do you say?" A note of desperation was slipping into his voice. *If I don't reel him in some he might slip the hook.*

"Do you have a doorman?" I asked coquettishly.

"Well, no. My apartment is not that fancy. But it did at one time, so I'm told." Hope was slipping back into his voice.

"How far is your apartment?" I was getting ready to sink the hook in, like my husband taught me while introducing me to his fishing hobby.

"It's just three blocks around the corner." He was beginning to almost glow with the possibilities running through his mind.

"Let's go." Isabella noted that her dinner was already starting to season nicely.

127

The apartment really was very nice. As Isabella walked in, she first noted the fireplace as the center point of an entertainment center that contained a TV to the left with an impressive looking stereo system just over the TV. To the right of the fireplace was something of a library of hard- and soft-covered books. To her right was a kitchen nook and on the nook was a wine rack almost full of various wine bottles. *Well, at least he had not lied about having wine to drink.* The wine rack's quality and richness was of no concern to her. She was really not here to dine ... on wine.

"Would you like to get comfortable while I get the fire going? Then I will pick a nice wine for us to enjoy"

I can smell your juices flowing already, Mr. Phil Bowman. Dinner is simmering.

"Actually, I was about to ask for directions to the little girl's room," Isabella answered, slipping a little shyness into her act.

"Sure, sure ... it's just past the kitchen, first door on your left as you enter the hallway. If you should miss it, you will end up in my bedroom."

Was that a blush blooming on your checks? Don't tell me you are a virgin, Mr. Bowman. This could really be one special holiday dinner.

Isabella almost purred, "Play your cards right, and we might just end up in there anyway." That got his heart pumping and smell of the endorphins starting to flow as well. She left him, her ass waving sensuously to head in to the "little girl's room" while considering a real surprise that would be in store for him before the evening's end.

In the lavatory, Isabella freshened up and removed her dress to display a little, black, baby doll number that would surely get his endorphins surging, if it doesn't give him a heart attack first. She recalled how she actually did have a client die of a heart attack while feeding on him. The old man just got too excited. She had fed to her fill and left him dead in that dive of an apartment room that one rents by the hour, instead of by the night. When she left, she had made a point of enthralling the bellman who took their money and gave them the key to the room so he would not be able to remember her when the constables came.

As she was leaving the room, she noticed that the door had a full-length mirror that showed nothing of herself, not even the way the nightie separated ever so slightly in the middle to nicely display her sexy black panties and her long, luscious bare legs. She was confident that if her legs were not as young and muscular looking as they felt, to her gentleman they would truly appear to be, due to her supernatural magic.

When she entered the living room, she was disappointed not to find the man there to enjoy her surprise entrance. A voice from the kitchen announced, "I'll be there soon. I can't find the corkscrew for the wine."

As the noise of his routing around in the kitchen continued, she started looking at the titles of the books on the shelf. He had a large collection of horror and science fiction books, including a section of vampire tales. One of the hardbacks was entitled, "The Blood Countess." She removed that from the shelf and found a picture of herself on the cover. It was an old picture, truly, from back in her living days. She remembered the long hours sitting for the large oil painting that was this cover art. She slipped the book beside her purse on the couch. She called out to the man in the kitchen, "Have you read this entire book collection on your library shelves?"

"Not all, but most."

"What about all these vampire books?" she asked.

"Oh yes, especially the vampire books, I'm a big fan of vampires." He continued his rummaging while yelling out from the kitchen.

"Phil, forget about the corkscrew. I really did not come for the wine," Isabella announced. She quickly walked over to the couch that faced the kitchen so he would see her as he entered into the room from the hallway. He had not yet seen her, as the kitchen entrance had saloon-like bat doors, and he had been busy as she walked by the kitchen. Isabella made a point of not crossing her legs as he walked in. Now was not the time to be demure.

As she waited for the entrance of her holiday meal, she noted that the fireplace was going, but she also noted that it was a false fireplace with a real fire burning within, she could smell the gas and hear the gas flowing, most likely a human would notice neither, noted both through her heightened vampire senses. Phil had probably started it with a flick of a switch. It did give off a nice warm glow, while giving warmth to the room, giving a feeling of a real fireplace.

Just then Phil entered the room. When he saw Isabella, she thought he was about to faint. *I guess this nightie still has it.* Isabella noted that Phil had removed his suit coat, tie and had unbuttoned his shirt halfway down his chest. He had a very hairy chest. *What a turnoff.* He still looked as if he was going to faint, so Isabella instructed, "Phil, why don't you come sit beside me."

Isabella was planning to make a nice evening of it until he showed off that horrid, hairy chest. When Phil started to come to her, she asked, "Phil, dear, please bring me that book on the other couch, the one sitting next to my purse." He did as requested just like a faithful servant.

Once he got seated, she noted that his heart was beating very hard. She figured that his endorphins were just gushing through his system, but Isabella thought, *I'll try to season my dinner just a little more.* "Phil, look at the book cover and tell me what you see."

He obeyed as a well-trained servant. He started in with, "This is a great read. It's all about this crazy bitch who tries staying young by killing off virgins and bathing in their blood."

"Yes dear, but look more closely at the cover, and tell me what you see," Isabella said more commandingly.

He looked at the cover of the book, then looked at Isabella. "You know, if you put your hair up, you would look a lot like this cover picture."

As he studied her face, Isabella smiled and let her fangs extract. Phil looked as if he was truly going to faint. That would not have ruined her dinner, but some of the seasoning would have been lost, so she ordered in her best enthrall voice, "Do not faint."

He did not faint.

As a look of total horror contorted his face, Isabella slipped in close and kissed him. He shivered in shock. She moved her lips down, to the side of his neck, oh so lightly. Phil started shivering like a man with the black plague. Actually, he was just reacting to being a highly-seasoned dinner – endorphin and adrenaline overload for him, fine seasoning for her.

Isabella so slowly, almost lovingly, slipped her fangs into his neck and began to shake in orgasmic pleasure as Phil's properly seasoned blood gushed down her throat. He gushed so freely that she almost choked on the pure pleasure of tonight's holiday meal.

After Isabella had her fill of Phil, she shoved his drained, lifeless corpse aside to drop down onto the couch, where the momentum made him roll over and flop on the floor at her feet. After that slightly painful comment about "the crazy bitch" on the cover of her book, she had lost interest in Phil for anything but dinner.

Originally, Isabella's plans called for a night of multiple dining, all possible without doing any killing. Phil had changed those plans. Phil was so delightfully filling. It was too early to head back to her room, so she chose to enjoy the fake fire and read a good book about herself.

Chapter Seventeen
The Mole is Back

After some very pleasant horizontal exercise with my wife, I rolled over for a bit of a nap. My tripping to dreamland was interrupted with Di feeling my back. *Hasn't that girl had enough?*

"Jack, your mole is coming back." Diana's voice was filled with concern.

I could sense her anxiety, so I answered the concern in her voice, "The doctor said that was a possibility. I'll just set up another appointment and have it removed again."

The next day, I did set up an appointment with the dermatologist. Having gone through having one mole removed, I was the cool, experienced one this time. I set up the appointment for a Friday afternoon in hopes that Diana could start her weekend a few hours early and take me to this appointment. My plans turned out to be workable with Di.

Thursday evening the phone rang. I decided to let one of the sisters (Di or Chris) get it, as I was getting to a really good climax to the audio book I had been listening to for days. The vampire of this tale, a real she-beast was about to get hers.

The great climactic ending was interrupted with Di calling down the stairs, "Jack, it's your dermatologist on the phone. The doctor wants to talk to *you*."

"OK." The phone was in easy reach, so all I had to do was turn off the audio book machine, pick up the phone and hit a big button that I recalled had "TALK' on it. "Hello, this is Jack."

"Jack, this is Dr. Peterson. I understand you have an appointment with me tomorrow afternoon pertaining to a reemerging mole. Is that right?"

"Yes."

"If you can, I would like you to come down to the lab and have some blood work done. Today is Wednesday, and on Thursdays the lab is open evenings until 10 p.m. If you can get to the lab today, I'll set it up so that I will have the results in my possession before you arrive for your appointment tomorrow afternoon."

Diana, still on the phone answered, "I can drive him down right now."

I thought, *That's my girl,* but what I said was, "I'll go get the blood tests done and see you tomorrow, doc."

"Fine, until then, have a good evening."

Right, a good evening sitting around the waiting room of the lab for an hour or two, then getting needled. I considered taking my audio book with me, but I hate earplugs, and people sitting around me might not have a strong enough stomach to overhear this great vampire tale. As Di called down, "Ready to go?" I decided to leave the book behind.

"Coming," I called back.

Luckily, we only had to sit around for about an hour before I was called in to have blood taken. Di spent the time keeping Elaine happy. Chris had volunteered to watch Elaine while we were out, but Di wanted to take Elaine along, to give Di something to do in the waiting room.

When I was called in to "the Vampire Room,' my favorite name for the room where blood is taken, the med-techs were quick, proficient and almost painless—but not quite.

Chapter Eighteen
Dr. Peterson

The next day I was on time for my appointment. I was trying to play it cool, but Diana kept sharing horror stories that friends at church and at work had told her, stories with the person going through hellish treatments only to die of cancer anyway. I know my loving with meant well but too much information right now.

Eventually, my wife's string of loving nightmares ended with the nurse summoning me to see the doctor.

As I walked up to the door, I heard the nurse's voice so I asked, "OK if I take your shoulder?"

Taking my outstretched hand and placing it on her shoulder, she answered, "No problem." She led me down two hallways to an empty exam room. I couldn't help but notice that the nurses were getting quite proficient at leading me around. I also noticed that this nurse had no bra strap under her uniform or under my touch.

After the usual taking of my blood pressure, temperature, and pulse, Dr. Peterson finally made his appearance. He waited until he sat down before he said anything. This was not a good sign. "Mr. Poisner, you have signs of melanoma in your blood tests. This means that you must likely have stage IV melanoma. Stage IV is the hardest type to treat." He paused to let that information sink in, and then he continued, "What we need to do now is to get you into a hospital for a total body scan to see where and how far the melanoma may have spread. I feel I must tell you this up front. The fact that the melanoma is spreading through your blood instead of through your lymph nodes is a very bad sign. BUT, don't be picking out coffins just yet. Let us perform some hospital tests and see what we shall see. Any questions?"

"Yes, what about treatment? How long have I (the words "to live" choked in my throat and never made it out)?" That was just two of a mass of swarming questions I could grab hold of and put to words.

"Let's just wait on that until after the body scans are available. Any other questions?"

I was a little too freaked to verbalize any of the other questions tumbling over each other in my mind for now, "No. I guess we will just have to wait to see those hospital tests. When will that be done?"

"I'll have to make some calls and see when the machine is free. I will get in touch with you as soon as possible, but it may take a few days. How did you get to your appointment?"

"My wife brought me."

"Would you like me to get a nurse to bring her in so I can discuss this with her?"

Recalling all the horror stories she was just sharing with me, I answered, "No. I'd really like to keep this cool until we know more from the tests. Friends have already filled my wife with doom and gloom stories. I'd rather wait until we know more before bringing her into this."

"OK. Do you need me to help you back out to the waiting area?"

"Yes, please." So he did. By now I could normally find my way out on my own, but for some reason I just felt too mentally numb to do so this time.

On the way home, Diana had lots of questions, but I kept to my guns that I should wait until after the hospital tests to begin to worry her. I kept to my guns until we got home. After she put the baby to bed for a nap, she walked into the bedroom and announced, "Spill it. What did the doctor have to say?"

I spilled the beans. I told her of the doctor's suspicions that I had cancer, but we would not know more until after I went to a hospital for additional body scans. With a forced tone of joviality, I made a point to mention the doc's comment on not going out looking for a coffin. That may have been a mistake. By the catch in her breathing, I don't think she was persuaded to stay calm until after the tests.

Tim Forder

I did share the stage IV diagnoses with Eric, and my concerns about the hellish treatments. When I added my thoughts of putting off the treatment, he could not pass up making me feel better by reminding me that his mother died of brain tumors as a result of her stage IV melanoma. When he started getting a bit too graphic as to what I might have to look forward to, I cut him off so I could try to get some sleep between now and the hospital test results.

I failed—another sleepless night.

Chapter Nineteen
Nuts

Paperwork, it never ends. There was a quiet presence in the office doorway, almost like that of a ninja (Have I seen too many of these imports?) *He'd better have a really good reason for interrupting or...*

Looking up from my paperwork, I said, "Mr. Masterson, this must be a first, you coming to my office instead of requesting I see you in your plush owner's office." Isabella had choked down the first impulse to give the intruder a good verbal beating for interrupting her paperwork. *Who are you kidding? You'd be tempted to give the intruder a raise for intruding your paperwork grief. But this is the boss; this has to be bad news.*

He disrupted her musings...

"Remember the plumbing work in the ladies' room, right next to my office? All that banging is giving me a headache."

"Would you like to use my office? I can get back to this paperwork after you are done here."

"Thank you, but I will be leaving soon. First I have some business to discuss with you."

I just know this is going to be bad news...

"The other owners and I are getting very concerned over the recurring police presence required here during the showing of the import movies." Pausing to let that sink in, he continued, "Don't get me wrong. You are doing a great managing job. You're handling these flare-ups very well, and we realize the problem is the violent nature of the imported movies. There has been a constant need for police presence AND the homicide department due to a number of killings around the theatre. Some of these homicides seem to have been customers who were killed after watching one of these imported movies here. Well, I thought I had to warn you that there is some discussion."

Just then the door crashed open.

Jeff started in, but when he saw the boss with her boss, he visibly froze, possibly pondering if he just blundered into losing his job.

"Well, what is it, boy?" Mr. Masterson orders.

"We have nuts in the theatre," Jeff almost stammers.

"Nuts?" Mr. Masterson asks, perplexed.

Isabella explained, "Nuts. This is a code for a customer using or flashing nunchucks in the theatre." She turned her attention back to Jeff, "Red nuts?"

"I'm afraid so," Jeff answered.

Getting into action by rushing out from behind the desk, "911 has been called?"

"Yes, ma'am, Ben is placing the call now."

With Mr. Masterson's concerns put aside for now, Isabella rushed out of the office with Jeff in front for about a pace or two, then she quickly left him behind.

As she rushed into the theatre, she saw a full blown mob scene with a group trying to rush not one, but two "nuts." One was currently in the act of smacking a would-be hero in the side of the head. As Isabella ran in and saw what was happening, the would-be hero dropped like so much lumber piling up at the feet of the "nuts." Currently the second "nut" was content in just standing by, waving his nunchucks around and around his body, showing off.

Using her best enthrall voice, she commanded, "This stops now."

On her command, the mob scene turned into a freeze frame. This freeze frame, which included both "nuts," ceased their dangerous actions.

The more dangerous "nut," the one who wasn't just standing around showing off, challenged her, "You want some of this?" The mob backed off with the relief of seeing some authority intervening into this hazardous situation.

Deliberately keeping eye contact with both "nuts," she approached slowly like a snake considering its next meal, slowly, cautiously, but in command. The two just stood watching her every move as she kept moving in, showing by her approach that she was the one in command.

The enthralled silence was interrupted by the audible intrusion of sirens from forthcoming law enforcement, EMS or both.

With the help of the audible distraction, the enthrall ended. The lumber jack of bloody bodies jumped over his log pile of downed bodies, with the full intent of making Isabella yet another (dead?) log for his pile. He brought his weapon down on her head.

Isabella, timing it right, just stepped to the side. She reached out and grabbed the weapon on its downward arc, originally intended to cleave her head in two. The action of Isabella grabbing the weapon with one hand surprised the nut. With her supernatural quickness it was quite easy to pull the weapon out of the "nuts" grasp. With the "nut" frozen in shock it was even easier work to karate chop him into unconsciousness, more lumber for the floor.

With a war yell the second "nut" announces his intent to avenge his fellow nut. Again Isabella moves to the side as the weapon comes down on nothing. This unexpected follow-through, making contact with nothing, leaves the "nut" off balance. It was no effort for Isabella to trip his legs out from under him. As he becomes yet more lumber for the floor, Isabella gives him a careful kick to the head meant to put him into dreamland, not to kill. She has no qualms about killing this trouble to her evening's movie events, but the law might frown on her over-doing their job. When she heard the sound of rushing feet from her blind side, she turns ready for battle only to find Jeff rushing to her side, excitedly proclaiming in his youthful exuberance, "Miss Báthory, how is your hand? Is it broken? Is it all right? Do you need EMS to look at your hand?"

"Jeff, calm down. My hand is just fine. (on second thought), well, it is a little painful but I am sure it is still in one piece."

"But I saw that nunchuck smack into the palm of your hand. How is it your hand isn't broken from such an impact?"

"Simple trick, really. As the nunchuck closed on my hand I pulled my hand back while grabbing the weapon, hence lessening the blow." This explanation seemed to quiet Jeff's questioning mind and leaves him in further awe of his boss.

With the danger subdued, Isabella looked over Jeff's shoulder to see Mr. Masterson standing at the theatre doorway. By the look on his face, this job is more likely deader than the two "nuts" she just put in dreamland.

The sirens proclaimed the onset of help just keep getting closer. *Are they screaming out the end of my employment?*

Chapter Twenty
A Death in the Family

A scream from the ground floor destroyed Jack's fitful slumber, "Jack. ... My god, JACK. Please, for God's sake wake up and get down here."

"OK, I'm coming," I yelled out to the walls, floor and open doorway, especially the open doorway. *Somebody had better have just died, waking me like this.*

Grudgingly I got up, walked over to my chair valet, grabbed a warm-up suit off the chair and shoes from under the chair. Reluctantly, and still waking up, I moved out of the bedroom, and headed down the stairs. I was surprised that Elaine hadn't awakened, with all this yelling going on. As I was going down the stairs, I thought, *All this had better not be over another spider or daddy-long-legs or I swear someone is going to die."*

When I entered the living room, Di grabbed my arm and pulled me into the dining room. She spun me so that I was facing the hallway which led to her sister's room.

"Di. What is this all about?" I asked still groggy from my rude awakening.

"Go. Go down the hall into Chris's room and see for yourself."

I was tempted to say, "See what? I'm blind," but this did not seem to be a good time for joviality. Something had really gotten Di spooked. It was starting to get me spooked as well, and I did not even know why."

I walked down to Chris's room as ordered, *I wish I could remember Chris's room's layout better, haven't seen her room in years. Maybe I should have asked Di for some visual help- nope, for what very reason,*

141

she obviously wanted me to come down alone and is clearly upset about something. With my mind too much on my thoughts I bumped my shoulder lightly against a door frame, I realized that I had arrived a few feet sooner than I had expected. It's been years since I have even looked into Chris's room let alone walked in.

"Chris? Chris, is everything alright?" I asked, tentatively.

No answer.

Not a good sign. Feeling as if I was walking into a morgue, I made a point of remembering the room layout, Chris's bed would be about 10 o'clock to her doorway, about four feet to the forward left. Cautiously I enter the room and walked toward the direction I believed the bed to be in, cautiously because, from my visual days, I recalled that Chris did not have the neatest bedroom around, then neither does her sister. Possibly this disaster area décor was a family thing.

Bumping into the bed, I gently moved my hand down and forward until I encountered cold, deadly cold (?) skin. *Please, not dead skin,* I silently prayed. Moving my hand, I quickly realized that it was Chris's wrist that I had found, and it was cold, all too cold. Out of reflex, I flinched. Forcing myself, I moved my hand up her cold death-like arm to her shoulder. From her shoulder, I found my way to her neck, and from her neck I felt my way to her slightly parted lips—the whole time my skin is crawling at the unnatural coolness of her skin. I also realized that during the whole time I had been feeling her body, she had not made a single noise or movement in protest. *Really a bad sign.*

Against all judgment that was screaming "turn and run away" I moved my hand up to her nose and felt—nothing, no feeling of breathing at all. I just couldn't let that be the final ruling, so I moved my other hand down to her chest to feel for movement, for any sign of breathing–and I found none.

"Is she ... is she..." Di interrupted my investigation.

Hmmm, here I thought Di too upset to come down here, keeping her from having to finish her sentence, even if she could. "I believe so." Then I realized that I had failed to finish the sentence. I assumed from Di's silence she got the message.

On a whim, I brought my hand up from her unmoving chest and felt the side of her neck...

"What ... what are you doing?" Di asked.

"Feeling for a pulse," I lied. What I found were two punched marks on the side of the neck, like a snake would make except for being too far apart—*more like a vampire would make.*

Di asked, shakily, "What should we do?"

"I guess, call the police," I answered.

"Is that necessary? You know she had a possible heart problem."

No, I did not know that she had a possible heart problem. "What is this about a heart problem?" I asked, a little disturbed at this sudden enlightenment.

"I thought I told you. Chris has been having some medical problems, so I had been taking her to see her doctor. Why, just last week, Chris went through a number of medical tests on her heart. In fact, I was trying to wake her so that we'd make her doctor appointment later today. We were supposed to see her doctor for the results of those tests."

"Maybe before we call the police we should call her doctor and see what he has to say."

"I'll do that right now." I heard Di rush down the hallway already going for the dining room phone.

I went back upstairs, not to resume my sleep, but to change from my leisurely warm-up suit to my street clothes. It looked like we'd be going out today.

While I was changing into my street clothes it occurred, not for the first time, that this was now a more difficult job then I had planned for originally. Back then, preparing for the most likely chance of going blind, I began changing my wardrobe to all white shirts with my pants in navy blue or black. I figured I would have no problem if and when I couldn't see to dress, if all my clothes were in the same color scheme. Of course, after we married, my loving wife insisted in putting color back into my wardrobe. Her loving logic was, "I'll always be there to help you pick out your shirts and pants and make sure you are color coordinated. Right. Now I have to feel for a Braille tab with the basic color of my clothes on the labels. As for my socks, they are still all basic navy blue. All my shoes were black, except for my tennis shoes (it's easy enough to feel the difference between my work or dress shoes and my soft-sided tennis shoes).

I turned at the sound of Diana walking into the room, "So Di, did you get to talk with Chris's doctor? If so, what did he have to say?"

In a sad tone I heard, "Yes. First I got his secretary, receptionist, whatever, who put his nurse on the phone. She got the doctor on the phone. He was not surprised at the news. When we were to see him today he was going to recommend putting her into the hospital for additional tests, possibly leading to some surgery."

She continued, "He asked that I call him back when we have a funeral home for her and his nurse would see that a fax of a signed death certificate be sent there. Should we call your father?"

"I was thinking the same thing, with Dad working at a funeral home and all. He should be lots of help."

"Will you call? I don't think I could make another phone call," she asked with her voice trailing off.

"No problem." *I hope.* I wasn't exactly feeling non-emotional about the loss of my sister-in-law, but I had to keep my cool for Diana's sake.

I called dad from the bedroom phone so Di could hear something of the conversation, if only my half of the conversation.

Mom answered. *Great, this is difficult enough.* "Hi, Mom. Is Dad home?"

"No he's at work. Is there a problem? Your voice is sounding strange."

I really can't get into this with mom. "Please give me his work number. I'll let him explain later. Right now I really need his work phone number. I really need to talk to Dad." I was hoping that Mom got the message how desperately I needed to talk to Dad.

"Jack, something is wrong."

Cutting her off, I replied, "Mom, I really can't get into this right now. Please give me the phone number."

She gave it to me.

I did not realize that I had just hung up on my mother until right after I did it. Now she's going to know something is wrong. I am never so rude as to just hang up on my mother.

I called the phone number for Universal Funeral Home, and explained to the person who answered that I was James Poisner's son and needed to talk to him. I finished with "… it's important."

"Unfortunately, your father is presently driving the hearse to the carwash, but he is due back anytime now." As my heart sunk at having to wait until later to talk to Dad, the gentleman said, "What do you know, the hearse is driving in as we speak. It just drove past the front window. He will be parking it in the back, and coming in the back door, just hold a second and I'll get him for you."

It seemed like a black hole in time had passed, then I heard what might be the phone being picked up and a very familiar voice said, "Son, is everything alright?"

I barely croaked out, "Chris is dead."

"What happened?"

"Heart attack." was all I could get out.

"Are you alright? How's Diana?"

"We're managing." Short answers seemed to be the best I could handle right now.

"I'm sure you are. You just take care of your wife, and I'll see to the rest.... Son, have you done anything about a death certificate?"

"Di, give me that phone number for her doctor."

She did, slowly and carefully. I put the ear to the phone preparing to pass it on when I heard, "I got it.... Hold one quick minute." I heard muffled voices, but could not hear what was being said.

I heard Dad get back on the phone, "OK. Mr. Roth, the man who answered the phone, will see to the death certificate. Another fellow whom you don't know will be coming with me, and we will be right out with the hearse to see to Chris's remains. You just keep cool, see to your wife and I'll see to everything else. See you soon." The phone clicked dead.

Hanging up the phone, I slid closer to Diana, put my arm around her and, following her example, sat quietly in our bedroom until we heard a knock at the front door.

When I answered the front door, an all familiar voice spoke. "It's your Dad." His voice then raised a little to talk over my shoulder, "Hi, Diana." She must have come out of the bedroom to stand at the top of the stairs. His voice changed, so I realized he was back to talking to me, "Mind my asking what you two were doing just before I knocked?"

"We were sitting upstairs on the bed."

"Tell you what. Why don't you and Diana go back into the bedroom while Mr. Parker and I get Chris into the hearse. It might be better if you two don't watch us removing her. You'll see her again at the funeral home."

I did as suggested. For an unknown time, we just sat quietly on the bed listening to the sounds of movement downstairs. It did not miss my attention that sweet baby Elaine was angelically sleeping through the whole thing. Finally, Dad called up, "Would you two mind coming down now."

As we did, Dad continued, "Mr. Parker's out in the hearse. Diana, dear, would you like me to drive you two over to the funeral home?"

"No, thanks. I can drive ... if Jack knows where it is." Di answered.

"Sure, it's easy. Just drive down Georgia Avenue turn left onto University and after a couple of miles look for the funeral home on the right side, right Dad?"

"That will get you there," Dad answered trying to sound upbeat.

"Oh, what about the baby?" Diana asked. "She's been sleeping through all this." Diana spoke from right behind me. I never even heard her come down the stairs.

"Got you covered. Grandma should be on her way here right now to stay with her little bundle of joy. If you're sure you feel up to driving, I will take off with Mr. Parker. *My* bundle of joy should be along soon." Before leaving, I heard him give Diana a good-bye hug for support. He then grabbed my shoulder, giving me a squeeze of comfort on the way out.

I was still standing by the front door beside Diana when from a distance I heard Dad call out, "There she is, coming down the road right now. We're going to take off so she's got a place to park in front of your house."

It was only minutes after I heard Dad get into the hearse and drive off that I heard another car drive up and park where the hearse had been, from the sound of it.

Soon after, we were on the road to the funeral home. Later, we were told that our little sleepyhead continued to sleep so long that her Nana, who sleeps better on the floor because of a bad back, laid a blanket on the floor and went to sleep right next to the crib. Our little one eventually woke up to the surprise of finding her Nana asleep on the floor next to her. That was the end of Nana's rest.

Back at the funeral home we had a busy day picking out a coffin for Chris, so that there could be a viewing here in Maryland for her Maryland friends. We made arrangements to have her transported up to Ohio for a viewing for her Ohio friends and family. After the viewings, she would be put to rest in a spot her mother had purchased for her so she would have her resting right next to her mother. The whole time we were busy making plans, I was expecting things to come to a halt with an announcement that the mortician, in doing his job, has discovered a strange lack of blood and two strange punch marks on the neck.

The more the planning went on, the more anxious I got that the planning was going to be brought to a close by the presence of homicide cops. Surprisingly, everything went well, but not surprising considering my father was right there to assist and advise throughout.

During the whole time those two punch marks nagged at my conscience. Eventually, with everything going so well, I was finding myself really temped to pull the pin on everything and request an examination of Chris's throat. Perhaps it was guilt for knowingly harboring a creature of death in my own home—a vampire who had killed a member of my family within my own home. I probably would have pulled the pin, but the other thing that nagged me was Eric's comment, "You and I may be horror nerds enough to possibly believe in the existence of vampires, but the authorities—not likely. Next you will be talking to the men with the long-sleeved white coats."

I was also reminded that even Eric did not believe that Isabella could be a vampire until he failed to see her in those glossy shields of my old watchband. Even then, he had to be persuaded that this was not some strange visual oddity of the shields. No, not wanting to be visited by the Sigmund Freud's and fitted for a straightjacket, I kept my peace. But how was it that Chris was being prepared by the mortician, and he was failing to take notice of the lack of blood and the puncture marks on her throat?

The more these oddities went undiscovered, the more I felt it was up to me to do something myself. After all, Isabella had to be the one who killed Chris. For whatever reason, could Di, the baby or I be next? *What was it Eric said about her not shitting where she lives? I guess Eric can't always be right. So who is she going to shit on next?*

After all the funeral arrangements for both Maryland and Ohio had been planned and everything was in the works that could be in the works, it was time to head back home.

While riding home, my mind was racing. Why did Isabella kill Chris? Could the rest of the family be next? If not the whole family, then who? Something had to be done, and there seemed to be only one person who could do it. Jack Poisner, the blind vampire hunter; Jack Poisner, the blind vampire killer.

Diana interrupted my mind bending exercise with, "Isabella doesn't know what happened. I guess I'll have to tell her."

"NO. I mean, I was just thinking that tonight you and the baby might feel better of spending the night at Eric's and Patty's, at least for the night. You're not going to want to spend the night in the house..."

Diana interrupted, "You're right, but don't you think someone should tell Isabella what has happened? Oh no, it's too late. By the time we get home, she'll have already gone to work." *I'm sure she already knows.*

Oh, shit! The baby and Nana. Shit, shit, shit, when that damn vampire woke up, could she have continued her rampage through the family?! Baby... No, wait. If she wanted to kill the whole family, she could have already. Nooo, she must have been after Chris only.

I answered Di's question with, "I'll stay in the house through the night and talk to Isabella when she arrives home from work in the morning."

"But hon', you two don't exactly get along."

"Don't worry. You have enough on your plate right now." *I will stay home and tell Isabella that I know what she did.* I continued my conversation with, "I will stay home, and when she returns from work, I will tell Isabella what has happened. I will also explain that you are staying next door for a while," I lied.

It was hours later, and I was still very awake. I didn't know how Diana might be sleeping through the night, but I knew I could not sleep, but not for the same reason. Diana may or may not have slept with a mind racing with thoughts of her sister, and the finish line being the final rest for her sister in Ohio. On the other hand, I could not sleep because my mind was busy preparing to confront Elizabeth Báthory, Blood Countess and Vampire.

Early on, I tried listening to my talking book, ironically yet another vampire tale, but I just could not keep my distracted mind on the story. I eventually gave up on listening to the vampire tale. It was just not talking to me. After all, why listen to a vampire tale when you're living a real life vampire tale. I spent most of the night with the stereo on, but not even Meat Loaf, Madonna, or the Beatles could keep my mind off the early-morning confrontation to come.

Eventually, it got to be time for the early-morning news, so I turned off the stereo and turned on the TV. I was coming to the realization that I was paying less attention to the news than I had been to my talking book. After all, it was getting close to the time when Isabella would be coming through the front door. It was getting close to the time for our final confrontation! My pulse was racing with fear at the thought of this impending confrontation with a real vampire, and not just any vampire, but the legendary Elizabeth Báthory, herself. I was assuming that Eric was right about her my boarder's linage.

You had better get your nervous fear under control, or you're going to give that Vampire the upper hand, like she doesn't already have it. Get it under control, or it could ruin your plans to protect your family. I feel as if I'm about to go into the dentist's office for a root canal.

Then it happened. I heard a key working the front door lock. It was time. The battle lines were about to be drawn. *Sounds as though she's having trouble with the lock again. I really have to look into fixing that lock soon, if I live long enough.* I could be a gentleman and go open the door for her, but for some reason, I just was not feeling very gallant right now.

As the door opened, I heard footsteps entering the house, and the room temperature dropped. I heard a voice from hell that said, "You are the only one home? Something is wrong?"

Like you don't know. I thought, but what I said was, "Diana and the baby are staying at a friend's." I made a point of not saying what friend.

"Why?" the voice from hell asked.

You know perfectly well why, you bloodthirsty killer. I answered with, "We had a death in the family. We found Chris dead in her bed this morning." I was fighting hard to keep my cool and to use my best matter-of-fact business voice.

"Oh, what happened to her? Does anyone know? Who found her?" She was trying to sound sincere, but coming from that hellish mouth, it was not working. She really did not have to sound sincere, as this battlefield only contained two combatants, and this blind vampire hunter knew the truth.

Maintaining my composure and my business tone, I continued, "Diana tried to wake her sister this morning in preparation for getting her to a doctor appointment. It seems she had a heart problem. Instead, we had to call her doctor to tell him that Chris was not going to make her appointment. When we informed him of Chris's ... condition, he was not surprised. With results from tests taken just last week in hand, Chris's doctor had planned to hospitalize Chris. He had planned for additional tests and very possibly surgery."

Silence followed.

Before that skin growling voice could speak again, I continued, "But we know what really killed her, don't we ... vampire."

"Excuse..."

"No excuse, vampire. Yes, I know who you really are, Elizabeth Báthory, Blood Countess and Vampire. I found your bite marks on the side of Chris's neck." With my composure lost, I nearly yelled out, or maybe I did yell out, *"You killed Chris!* Why? What danger could Chris possibly have been to you that you had to kill her?"

The skin crawling voice answered, "Since Halloween, she kept calling me by the name you are using for me. She kept calling me ... vampire."

"Big deal. She was mentally challenged. Who would have believed her?" I almost screamed for emphasis. I really was losing my composure, *Get under control, get under control for your family's sake.*

"Diana. I feared eventually Diana might listen to her sister and I would have to kill both Chris and my lovely Diana. I could hear Chris's heart problem, I could hear her heart laboring to function. I figured I could just take a little of her blood, not enough to be noticed, just enough to trigger her heart attack, all while she slept, with no one the wiser. But you, blind man, see more than others see, don't you? You, blind man, hear what others don't hear, don't you?"

"You mean that I hear your real voice, instead of the beloved voice everyone else hears? You failed to mention how the room temperature changes every time you walk into the room. With you in the room, it feels like being in a graveyard at night." I continued, "Mind telling me how you pulled it off? How does everyone see and hear some raving beauty instead of seeing and hearing the real you, the monster?"

"It bothers you that you almost have it all figured out, but not totally.... If I supplied you with an answer to your question, I doubt you'd believe me."

"I'm talking to a vampire, not any vampire, but the infamous Elizabeth Báthory, Blood Countess. I'd believe just about anything right now, don't you think?"

"In my travels, I spent some time in Greece. While there, I happened to come across a mermaid. Yes, blind man, a real mermaid. You humans can't see them unless they wish to be seen. Usually a mermaid is only seen when the mermaid or mermaids wish to taunt sailors to their death through the siren song and their magical flawless beauty. Humans who have seen a real mermaid tend not to live long enough to tell the tale. A few have, hence the folklore of mermaids. Since I am a supernatural creature akin to the mermaid, I could see them at will. I could see the mermaids as they really are, not as you humans see them. One night, when I came in contact with one, I gave the mermaid a choice of becoming my next meal or sharing her siren secrets with me. She chose to share her secrets. It seems their magical ability is similar enough to vampire enthrallment that I was able to put it to my use. Afterward, she was an interestingly different dinner. I don't often enjoy seafood."

"She gave you what you wanted, and you killed her anyway?" I asked in astonishment of her pure evil.

She continued, "Mermaids live in large family schools. It was just luck that I found this one alone. Would you want to live on an island with a large school of mermaids out for revenge? Would you like to live on an island surrounded by murderous mermaids just out to kill off the leak in their magical abilities by killing off the one who forced their magical secrets out of a family member?. No, her death was more for my survival than out of spiteful evil or a rare meal."

"So Vampire, are you now going to have to kill me, like you did Chris and that mermaid, to keep me silent?"

"You tell me. Am I going to have to kill you to keep my secret?" the sound of fingernails racking the blackboard asked. "Seems you have everything figured out, except I don't see any wooden stakes, and I'm willing to bet that glass of water on the coffee table is just drinking water and not holy water. Maybe you plan to keep talking until the sun comes up and gives me a burning sun tan. Oh, but Diana has the windows properly covered as I have instructed her, not with her knowledge, of course. She believes the window covering is her idea, to keep the baby from being sunburned while in the house."

I suddenly got an image from a Hammer Horror film where Van Helsing, confronted with his nemesis, Dracula, dived onto a table, dramatically slid across the polished table, and ripped down the large curtains covering a large set of windows. Dracula, suddenly trapped within the sun's rays, burned to death in the morning light. *I hadn't thought of the morning light. If I could burn her, would she burn to unrecognizable ashes? Would she burn to a point of removing the evidence of her demise? Who knows? It's risky, possibly suicidal, but I believe I have a better idea to save my loved ones from this bloodthirsty hell beast. Then again, if I survive ... yeah, right ... but if I do survive this confrontation with the blood countess, maybe I could get her out into the light of the backyard and let the sun burn away the evidence of my vampire hunting.*

"I see that idea had not occurred to you. Just as well. I would have noticed if the curtains had been tampered with and would have treated the situation accordingly. You don't think I have existed this long without having to outsmart a number of vampire hunters, do you?"

"How many vampire hunters have you ... on second thought never mind. You really don't think you're going to kill a member of my family, and I am not going to do something about it, *do you?*"

There was a wash of foul air, and suddenly, I was up off my feet as a machine like grip had me off the floor by my shirt, with a breath that smelled like a graveyard full of death, "And pray tell, what are you going to do to me..." she ended her question with a very mocking ... 'blind man.'"

The plan seemed to be working just fine so far. I choked out, "I am going to tell Diana just who you are..."

Everything suddenly came to a stop at the sound of a knock at the front door, and a voice gently calling out, "Jack, it's Eric. Are you up? Are you awake my man?"

The machine-like grip tightened so that even if I wanted to call out, I could not have.

There was an endless silence from the other side of the door. There were no more shout outs from Eric, no sounds of feet walking away—nothing. Then I heard a key put into the key hole, a key being put to use. *I don't recall hearing this bloodthirsty bitch closing, let alone locking the door. I guess I must have had my attentions too much on the coming battle.*

Then it hit me like a blow to the guts, *Oh, God, NO. Please don't let anyone come through that door. Please God.* My mind screamed as a vision of Diana and Eric coming through the door triggering a blood bath, a bloody bath of loved ones.

Eric or whoever it was with him trying to unlock the door was having problems. *I really have to get that lock fixed sometime soon.* I almost laughed inside myself. Then all hell did break loose...

Eric, the intruder into the battlefield, finally got the lock to work, and opened the door with a stage whisper, "Jack, you awa..." He looked into the room and saw Elizabeth Báthory with his best friend waving painfully in the air. Eric yelled out, "Let that man down." She did.

I suddenly found myself flying backward until I landed, crashing into the large screen TV and (worse) the TV table. Before I could shift my pain-racked mind back to anything but my screaming back, I heard an audible snap like a chicken being prepared to be dinner, *"Eric!"* I cried out. *That snapping sound just had to be Eric, Eric's neck, Eric's death. At least he died quickly, from the lack of a scream or any sound of resistance.*

A laughing voice from hell announced, "Sorry Jack, Eric is a little busy going to Hell right now. Shame to have ruined a perfectly good meal like that, simply snapping his neck like snapping a twig, but the way your adrenaline-laced blood is still pumping I'm sure you will be a pleasant repast." The voice was getting closer and the falling room temperature let me know that she was moving back toward me.

"Vampire, go to hell." It was not very original, but when you're hearing your death coming for you, what do you want.

Her laughing voice was hurting my ears, and I painfully heard her respond, "Been there. They threw me back."

Suddenly, that mechanically strong grip grabbed me off the floor as my injured back screamed in pain yet again.

Ignoring my back pain, I taunted, "So, is this were you go back to trying to bore me to death with your hellish peasant twaddle?"

"Peasant twaddle!" She all by screeched out. "I will remind you that I was once a countess. This was only my birthright as I was born into a family of nobles that even included kings. I have ruled over thousands. I don't speak peasant waddle. I roar with the nobility of generations."

"And now you are the junior manager of a third-rate movie theatre, during their graveyard shift," I continued to taunt.

"Enough."

It's about time I pissed her off enough to force her into action.

With a whiff of the breath of a demon passing my face, I suddenly felt her fangs sink deep into the side of my throat. It felt like my neck was being invaded by a couple of large dull needles. She wasn't bothering to be gentle. *Good, drink deeply, my dear demon.*

It was about time. She fell deeply into my trap.

As suddenly as she had invaded my neck, her attack ended just as abruptly, with my body flying backwards like the discarded rag doll of a spoiled brat. I hit the TV table again, screaming in back pain as I slumped to the floor. *If I survive this, my back will never be the same.*

She screeched out in a tone that was doing more than just threatening to hurt my ears, "What have you done to me?"

My words were grinning just as lively as I was, back pain, and all, "Going through a change of life, Vampire? Or should a say "a change of death?" Ever heard of a cancer called Melanoma? It's a nasty skin cancer that, once you get it, can kill you. You see, the cancer cells travel through your system to develop cancerous tumors all throughout your body. Severe Melanoma, like mine, can travel through the blood system....which is what I have."

I could hear her starting to strangle.

I continued, enjoying the sound of her discomfort. "Yes, my dear Blood Countess, you just ingested cancerous melanoma cells into your system."

"I have read of this," she interrupted, choking out, "It takes months or years to develop to such a deadly form."

"Yes, my dear Vampire. It takes a long time for melanoma to get so deadly in a human. But you are a Vampire with an extremely fast metabolism. Yes, Countess Elizabeth Báthory, your whole body is now developing cancerous tumors at such a fast pace that you can already feel your blood getting clogged by the cancerous cells traveling throughout your system. So what do you think will kill you first, brain tumors, lung cancer, or possibly blood clots that will stop the flow of your stolen blood, starving you to death?"

She started gagging...

Totally enjoying the sounds of her impending death, the gagging sounds gave Jack a thought. "Hmmm, maybe stomach cancer. Had not figured on that one."

Her horrid voice croaked out, "My head ... I have not felt ... such a headache since my living years." She croaked, "You have killed me, blind vampire hunter."

Her cold, deathlike hand reached to me, and I could feel lumps on her skeletal hand, lumps that were even now growing, lumps that Jack could feel moving and growing with much haste. *Tumors?* Then Jack heard the weight of her body hit the wooden living room floor.

Feeling downright giddy, I began wondering. *Dead? How can I tell? I can't feel for a pulse. Vampires don't have a pulse. Their circulatory system is too sluggish to feel their stolen blood pulsing through them. I can't feel for a heartbeat, which raises the question. If vampires don't have a working heart, how do they circulate their stolen blood? It was Eric who told me that vampires don't breathe, except to force air through their voice box to talk. Feel her skin? Hell no. Change in room temperature? She most likely would make the room temperature feel the same, dead or undead.*

Dummy, she is not trying to kill you. She must be dead.

That just was not good enough. Jack felt for her with his shoed foot. Once his foot bumped into what had to be her, he kicked out hard and felt the body move a little, but nothing more. *She must be dead.*

The war is over, and the blind vampire hunter is the winner. Now to call and explain all this to the cops.

Jack got up off the floor with his back still screaming like a banshee. He felt his way over to the dining room phone and punched, 911. An emotionless voice toned, "Police, Fire, or EMS?"

"Police," I answered.

"How can we be of assistance?"

Jack's mind went blank.

"Sir, how can we be of assistance?" the voice asked with more of a tone of urgency.

Jack discovered, just as he needed to think his mind was going numb on him.

"Sir..."

Jack interrupted with, "I want to report a murder."

After supplying some basic information such as his address, he quickly tired of playing twenty questions and hung up the phone. He found the closest dining room chair. After positioning the chair properly under his pain racked body, he dropped into the chair to await the arrival of the police.

Jack got to thinking. *I figured that what will follow would clear me of any prison charges. I'll just explain that my boarder and I were having a heated argument. After all, it was no secret that the two of us never really got along, so the reason for the argument really would not be important. Eric, my best bud from next door, came charging in with the assistance of a key that my wife must have provided him. Oh, my wife is staying next door currently grieving at the loss of her sister who apparently passed away during the night. She had a heart condition, you see. Anyway Eric came charging in and Isabella attacked him. It sounded like she broke his neck. In fact, she bragged about snapping his neck like a chicken being prepared for dinner. How could a little lady like her so easily break a grown man's neck? Why she's a master of kung fu. Her boss can verify that for you.*

What happened to Isabella? I don't know. She screamed in pain about a massive headache and just dropped to the floor. I believe she's dead, but I'm not a doctor.

Yes, the coroner will verify that Eric was killed by his neck being broken, very possibly by a kung fu attack. He will also verify that Isabella Báthory died of stage IV melanoma. Most likely he will verify that she died of brain tumors, blood clots, or whatever as a side effect of her melanoma.

"Eric...dear, dear old friend, Eric Van Helsing. How in heaven are you going to explain to your ancestors that you allowed yourself to be killed by a *Vampire?*"

Pleasant Nightmares.

NOTES

Adrenaline

A hormone produced by the body when you are frightened, angry, or excited, which makes the heart beat faster and prepares the body to react to danger
-Cambridge Dictionary Online

To a Vampire, adrenaline is one of two seasonings that make a good crimson protein meal into a great crimson protein meal. Created as a "fight or flight" survival mechanism, this is why many vampires like to fill their meal full of fear before consuming it, making for a nicely spicy dinner. The other spice of favor flavor is endorphins [See Notes: Endorphins]

Dumb Terminals

Dumb terminals were computer terminals that someone connected to a very large main computer. Most dumb terminals looked like advanced typewriters. Unlike future PCs that could do many things, dumb terminals could do nothing but connect you to one large computer system that did all the work as programmed. In contrast, early PCs were called smart terminals as the PC, not the mainframe, could do the work locally.

Dr. Who

Dr. Who was a low-budget BBC children's program that started airing in 1963. The plots told tales of a humanoid alien who traveled in time through the cosmos in a time machine that looked like a British Police Phone box called "The Tardis." From time to time, the alien went through changes in appearance, much like a snake sheds its skin. This allowed for the change in actors playing the good doctor over the many years it aired. New episodes can be seen even today on BBC and BBC America.

Elizabeth Báthory

If the name seems familiar, but you can't place it, or if the name does not seem familiar at all and you would just like to learn more about this legendary Blood Countess, I suggest you check out Vampire Owner's Manual.

Endorphin

Any of a group of proteins occurring in the brain and having pain-relieving properties typical of opium and related opiates. Discovered in the 1970s, they include encephalin, beta-endorphin, and dynorphin. Each is distributed in characteristic patterns throughout the nervous system. Endorphins released in response to pain sustained exertion causing, e.g., the "running's high". They are also believed to have a role in appetite control, release of pituitary sex hormones, and shock. There is strong evidence that they are connected with "pleasure centre's" in the brain.
-Merriam Webster (online) Dictionary

To a Vampire, endorphins is one of two seasonings that make a good crimson protein meal into a great crimson protein meal. Created during sexual arousal, this is why many vampires like to sexually entice their meal before consuming it, making for a nicely spicy dinner. The other spice of favor is adrenaline [See Notes: Adrenaline]

Legal Blindness

Legal blindness is defined by the Social Security Act of 1935 as; visual acuity for distance of 20/200 or less in the better eye after correction; or visual acuity of more than 20/200 if the widest diameter of visual field subtends an angle no greater than 20 degrees .
-Kirtly, Donald. *The Psychology of Blindness*. Chicago; Nelson-Hall, 1975.

Melanoma

Melanoma is very treatable if caught early. It does not have to be fatal. Remember this story takes place in the 80s. Treatment back then was a bit different than it is today.

Night Blindness

Night blindness is impaired vision in dim light and in the dark, due to impaired function of specific vision cells (namely, the rods) in the retina.

The ability of our eyes to quickly view objects as they shift from light to dark areas and the ability to see in dim light or at night is an important part of our visual health. When we are not able to do such, the condition is referred to commonly as night blindness or medically as nyctalopia. It occurs as a result of various diseases that cause degeneration of the rods of the retina (the sensory cells responsible for vision in dim light).
-MedicineNet.com

Peripheral vision

Peripheral vision is side vision, or the ability to see objects and movement outside of the direct line of vision.

Rods and cones are sensitive to color and work only by day; most of them are located in the center of the retina, but there are also cones in the periphery. Rods are responsible for night vision and low-light vision, but cannot distinguish color.
-MedicineNet.com

Sleep Apnea

Sleep apnea is the temporary stoppage of breathing during sleep, often resulting in daytime sleepiness. Apnea is a Greek word that means "want of breath."

The Blind Vampire Hunter

The most common form of sleep apnea is obstructive sleep apnea. In obstructive sleep apnea, the muscles of the soft palate around the base of the tongue and the uvula relax, obstructing the airway. The airway obstruction causes the level of oxygen in the blood to fall (hypoxia), increases the stress on the heart, elevates blood pressure, and prevents the patient from entering REM sleep, the restful and restorative stage of sleep. In other words, sleep apnea causes deprivation of quality sleep.

The symptoms of obstructive sleep apnea include loud snoring and/or an abnormal pattern of snoring with pauses and gasps for air. Other symptoms include excessive daytime sleepiness, memory changes, depression, and irritability. In some patients sleep apnea can contribute to high blood pressure, heart failure, stroke, and heart attack.
-MedicineNet.com

Common treatment after testing 1) weight loss, as being over-weight can be a direct cause of sleep apnea. Enough weight loss could possibly cure a case of sleep apnea. 2) The use of a CPAP machine. The CPAP forces air through your obstruction to your lungs at a fixed, predetermined rate. The predetermined rate is a direct result of professional sleep testing.

Use of a CPAP machine while sleeping has proven to be a very effective way of treating sleep apnea.

About the Author

Timothy (Tim) Forder was born and raised in Maryland, USA. It's my mother's theory that I get my love of horror and fantasy from being born just a couple of blocks from the gravesite of Edgar Allen Poe in Baltimore!

I'm a very happy family man with a family consisting of a beautiful wife, a creative teenage daughter, (live-in) sister-in-law, Seeing Eye Dog and daughter's rabbit.

For some years now, I have been losing what little eyesight I have left to RP (Retinitis Pigmentosa). If you need someone to talk to about coping with vision loss or Seeing Eye Dogs feel free to e-mail me at Facebook.

I have been a huge fan of the horror and fantasy genre, specially the older material, since my pre-teen years. I was introduced to the genre by the family sitter. Sue and I had an agreement: If I didn't beat up on my sister I could watch Creature Feature with her, which was past my bedtime and after my sister went to bed. I will never forget Sue Greenspan's words of wisdom: "Remember, what you see in the movies is only make believe and can't hurt you." Years later, I was the man when my buddies and I would go see Hammer Horror movies at the local theatre, and I would sit in my seat laughing at my friends as they tried to take cover from the horror on the screen! Sue Greenspan, if you are reading this thank you for many fun filled hours with my monsters!

Started my college studies in Wildlife Biology. I wrote a thesis on Dracula that was picked as the year's best work. I was given the honor of reading the thesis to the class, and by sundown, the paper was both famous and infamous around campus! As a result, on campus my nickname of "Tex" (because of my flare for western hats) became "The Vampire".

A bookworm from my early years, I still consume books like food, only being blind, most of my books are compliments of The Congressional Talking Book program (books on special cassettes or the newer digital books for the visually handicapped).

Other works by the author at Melange

The Lone Werewolf
Vampire Owner's Manual

www.ingramcontent.com/pod-product-compliance
Lightning Source LLC
Chambersburg PA
CBHW052136170626
46812CB00004B/1457